Will Carleton

City Festivals

Will Carleton

City Festivals

ISBN/EAN: 9783743330610

Manufactured in Europe, USA, Canada, Australia, Japa

Cover: Foto ©Andreas Hilbeck / pixelio.de

Manufactured and distributed by brebook publishing software
(www.brebook.com)

Will Carleton

City Festivals

"SARAH, LET ME LISTEN WHILE THE DRUMS MARCH BY."

BY

WILL CARLETON

AUTHOR OF

"FARM BALLADS" "FARM LEGENDS" "FARM FESTIVALS"
"CITY BALLADS" "CITY LEGENDS" ETC.

ILLUSTRATED

NEW YORK

HARPER & BROTHERS, FRANKLIN SQUARE

1892

TO

GOD, THE GREAT FATHER

TO

EARTH, THE GREAT MOTHER

AND TO

THE SUFFERING, SORROWING

REJOICING, CONQUERING, HUMAN RACE

ALL SISTERS AND BROTHERS

Preface.

IN this sixth and last book of the Farm and City Series, it may be appropriate for its author to mention the plan and theory which he has endeavored to make his guide throughout the work.

He believes, first, that the most important consideration of a book or a poem, so far as it is within the author's control, is the motive; which should be connected either with the substantial improvement, or the rational entertainment of the human race. The author who has the attention of any great number of people, and does not use it to make them better and truer, is to be pitied, as well as his readers.

Second, he believes that the next most important thing in a book or poem, is its spirit and feeling—the servant of the motive. This should be hearty, deep, and sincere. Whatever the feeling which the author strives to express, he must first experience himself, in order to communicate it to his readers. No writer can touch the heart of his audience, unless his own heart has first been touched. The only sure way to the brain is through the heart. Millions of volumes are to-day finger-deep in the dust of library-cemeteries, because their makers did not write them with their hearts—did not really mean what they said. And the public felt the lack, knew them for something it did not wish, and neglected them.

Third, he believes that the next most important consideration in a book or a poem is the subject-matter—the thought, the material—servant of the motive and feeling. This should never be above the comprehension of the average mind and thought of the world—if the author expects to write for the people in general, and not for the short-lived praises of a small, transient, artificial admiration-society. There is no thought so great, so complicated, so ineffably sublime, that it cannot be resolved into elements easily understood by the average human intellect. It should be the work of a poet, not to make plain thought or lack of thought complex and difficult of being understood, but to simplify and interpret nature and art to his readers; not to produce a series of rhymed riddles and enigmas, but epics, dramas, or lyrics such as the human race can understand, enjoy, and use, for their entertainment and instruction.

Fourth, the language of a book or poem—servant of the motive, thought, and feeling—should not be stilted or strained. An author ought not to consider that the moment he drops into rhyme, he must immediately rise again, in a balloon of polysyllabic words and incomprehensible phrases. The clearer the window-pane, the brighter may be seen the flowers of the garden and the tints of the sky as observed through it; and the simpler and more lucid the author's language, the more easily are observed and felt whatever beauty and power the thought may possess.

It is often allowable to introduce, to a certain extent, the dialect speech of some of the characters represented, on account of the directness, simplicity, and quaintness of language thus called into use. Still, dialect should not be employed unsparingly, or with the evident design of concealing the poverty of material by the queerness of the language, or with more lapses from the established rules than uneducated people naturally make (which are much less in number than one would suppose, before careful notice). The great mistake of many writers is, that they out-dialect dialect.

Fifth, come the various arts which are used in making a book or poem attractive or efficient; and all are commendable, if used, not to the injury, but to the aid of the foregoing qualities. There are the figures, which should be fresh, natural, and, as fully as possible, evolved from the author's own thought and observation; not mere reproductions from previous writers. So far as an author uses another's thoughts, figures, and expressions, either consciously or unconsciously, he is a compiler, and not an author. Figures should also be striking and apparent, and not so ineffably delicate as to require a literary microscope to detect them. There are the measures; which should be as regular and as conformable to established rules as the thought and feeling permit, but should not be made into jails in which to imprison and stifle sentiment and sense. There are the rhymes; which, if used, should be short, perfect, or extremely allowable, and, if possible, striking and felicitous. And there are many other generally admitted arts and expedients, which, like architecture with the casual observer, have more or less effect upon all readers of poetry, whether they understand them or not. But all these last are only the humble, though perhaps glittering, slaves of the qualities first mentioned; and when used without them, form dreary and pitiable exhibits.

These details of the poetical creed which the author has striven to follow during the preparation of these volumes, and from which he has often fallen far short, are given in hopes that some younger writers may recognize in them their own natural beliefs; that they may find in them a certain amount of help and guidance in their work. In regard to himself, he would say, that although he has not been able to adhere to them as closely as he could wish, yet one of the chief pleasures which his millions of readers afford him is, that they induce him to believe that he has, to some extent at least, succeeded in carrying out his own theories.

W. C.

Contents.

The Festival of the Freaks—*Including,*

The Festival of the Tram Club—*Including,*

The Festival of Family Reunion.

Notes.

Illustrations.

FESTIVALS OF THE NATION.

CITY FESTIVALS.

———◆———

𝕱estivals of the 𝕹ation.

I.

John Jones of Philadelphia was festively inclined;
Possessed obese anatomy and glad gregarious mind;
A man of wealthy bachelorhood; with gracious power and will
Quite happy oft to make himself and others happier still.
And every time a famous Yankee anniversary came,
Arrangements promptly he prepared to celebrate the same:
The January day when first Ben Franklin glanced upon
The Boston which acquired that day her most illustrious son;
The frigid February date when Washington first smiled
Upon the country that was yet to call itself his child;
The raw March day when Quakers made Concession's proclamation,'
Thus furnishing a germ and hint for our own Declaration;
The weeping April day when, with a baby voice's aid,
Young Thomas Jefferson his first free utterance loudly made;
The sweet May day on which, amid the tear-drops' fragrant showers,
War-mourners covered first the graves of those they loved with
        flowers;
The famous seventeenth day of June, when, with new-welded will,
Americans both lost and won The Battle of the Hill;
The sultry summer day when, set by passion's earthquake free,
A new-found nation showed its head above Oppression's sea;
The August day when Fulton first, without a stitch of sail,
Climbed up the Hudson's liquid stair, in Acclamation's gale;

The blithe September day this land has no right to forget,
That made America the gift of valiant La Fayette;
The gold October day in which Columbus bent the knee,
And thanked his God for showing him a refuge for the free;
The bright November day, when, driven by patriot endeavor,
Armed Britons trimmed reluctant sails, and left New York forever;
The bright December day on which the *Mayflower's* frozen band
Stepped on the famous Pilgrim Rock, and thence to Freedom's land;
And several other days that came into his heart and mind,
On which the western world had served the cause of humankind.

And this is how John Jones observed the thirtieth morn of May:
He gathered thirty veteran braves who loved the mournful day,
And strewed their banquet-hall with flowers; for, as he often said,
He did not like to have them wait for wreaths, till they were dead.

And when the banqueting was done, they held their glasses high,
In silent reverence, while they drank to comrades in the sky;
And then came speeches, songs, and rhymes, that bred the laugh and
    cheer,
Or called a gentle sadness forth, and many a silent tear;
And once a veteran, who could feel the words upon their way,
Recited this short monologue of Decoration Day:

HEAR THE DRUMS MARCH BY.

Sarah, Sarah, Sarah, hear the drums march by!
This is Decoration Day. Hurry, and be spry!
Wheel me to the window, girl; fling it open high!
Crippled of the body, now, and blinded of the eye,
Sarah, let me listen while the drums march by.

Hear 'em; how they roll! I can feel 'em in my soul.
Hear the beat—beat—o' the boots on the street;
Hear the sweet fife cut the air like a knife;
Hear the tones grand of the words of command;
Hear the walls nigh shout back their reply;
Sarah, Sarah, Sarah, hear the drums dance by!

Blind as a bat, I can see 'em for all that;
Old Colonel Ray, stately an' gray,
Riding, slow and solemn, at head of the column;
There's Major Bell, sober now, and well;
Old Lengthy Bragg, still a-bearing of the flag;
There's old Strong, that I tented with so long;
There's the whole crowd, hearty an' proud!
Hey, boys, say! can't you glance up this way?
Here's an old comrade, crippled now, and gray!
This is too much. Girl, throw me my crutch!
I can see—I can walk—I can march—I could fly!
No, I *won't* sit still an' let the boys march by!

Oh! I fall and I flinch; I can't go an inch!
No use to flutter; no use to try.
Where's my strength? Hunt down at the front;
There's where I left it. No need to sigh;
All the milk's spilt; there's no use to cry.
Plague o' these tears, and the moaning in my ears!
Part of a war is to suffer and to die;
I must sit still, and let the drums march by.

Part of a war is to suffer and to die—
Suffer and to die—suffer and to— Why!
Of all the crowd I just yelled at so loud,
There's hardly a one but is killed, dead, and gone!
All the old regiment, excepting only I,
Marched out of sight in the country of the night.
That was a spectre band went past so grand.
All the old boys are a-tenting in the sky—
Sarah, Sarah, Sarah, hear the drums moan by!

———

And then a girl arrayed in black, her eyes cast sadly down,
Rehearsed a veteran soldier's griefs, in words of Private Brown:

PRIVATE BROWN'S REFLECTIONS.

The gathered ranks with muffled drums had grandly marched away—
The hills had caught the sunset gleam of Decoration Day;

The orator had held the throng on sorrow's trembling verge,
The choir had sung their saddest strains—the band had played a dirge:
Some graves that had neglected been through many lonely hours,
Had leaped again to transient fame, and blossomed forth with flowers:
And one old veteran, Private Brown, with gray, uncovered head,
Still wandered 'mongst those small green hills that held his comrades
    dead.

He bent and stroked the humble mounds, with kind, old-fashioned word—
He called his comrades all by name, as if he knew they heard;
He said: "Ah, Private Johnny Smith! you lie so cold and still!
This isn't much like that summer day you spent at Malvern Hill!
The bellowing of the mighty guns your voice screamed loud above:
You yelled, 'Come on and see how men fight for the land they love!'
You furnished heart for fifty fights; and when the war was through,
You vainly hunted round for work a crippled man could do.
They let you die, with want and debt to be your winding sheet;
But this bouquet of flowers they sent, is very nice and sweet.

"Ah, Jimmy Jones! I recollect the day they brought you back:
They marched your body through the street, 'neath banners draped
    in black.
Your funeral sermon glittered well: it told how brave you died:
The tears your poor old mother shed, were partly tears of pride.
None left to-day to lean upon but country and her God,
She crept from yonder poor-house door to kiss that bit of sod.
It's hard, my boy, but nations all are likely to forget;
And God must take His own good time to make them pay a debt.
The sweet forget-me-nots that grow above your faithful breast,
Are types of His good memory, boy, and He knows what is best.

"Philander Johnson, from the plains we left you on as dead,
You carried to the prison-pen a keepsake made of lead;
You starved there for your country's good—at last you broke away,
And got in time to Gettysburg to help them save the day.
You hired a man to ask for you a pension, 'twould appear:
Your papers lost—they put you off from weary year to year
And when at last you took your less-than-thirty cents a day,
You had to fight to keep the law from taking it away.

"HE BENT AND STROKED THE HUMBLE MOUNDS, WITH KIND, OLD-FASHIONED WORD."

Some school-boy doctor every month must probe your aching side,
And thump you like a tenor drum, to find out if you lied.
You cost the Nation little, now—old hero of the fray—
It sent some very pretty flowers to strew you with to-day.

"Yes, Lemuel White; this little flag is all that's left to mark
The place where you retired so young, to chambers cold and dark.
The wooden slab I put up here so men your deeds could know,
Was broken down by sundry beasts, not many months ago.
But yonder monument upreared upon the village green,
Is partly yours, although your name is nowhere to be seen;
The country had your body, boy, it gives to God your soul;
It needed not your name except upon the muster roll!

"Forgive me, boys—forgive me, God! if I had blood display;
But flowers seem cheap to men whose hearts are aching day by day.
Forgive me, every woman true, whose tender, thrilling hand
Has lifted up to bless and soothe the saviors of the land.
Forgive me, every manly heart that knows the fearful strain
Of standing 'twixt America and blood and death and pain.
Forgive me, all who know enough to fight the future foe,
By doing justice to the ones who fought so long ago!
It is to those who trample us, that I feel called to say,
That flowers look cheap to those who starve and suffer day by day!"

  .   .   .   .

The sun had fallen out of view; the night came marching down;
The twinkle of the window-lights came creeping from the town.
The band was playing cheerful airs—glad voices decked the scene—
And dancing were the youths and maids upon the village green.
The gloomy graves were half forgot, and pleasure ruled the night;
But God has ways to teach us yet, that Private Brown was right.

————

And last of all for them was read, with martial tone and mien,
A tribute to the famous dead, and called,

2

OUR GUESTS UNSEEN.

Who are the guests in this festal throng?
    Many are here that we love and see:
Men who have heard the soprano song
    Of flying bullets that death set free;
Men who left a part of their days
    Off in the field where the blood stains are;
Men who had dropped the sweet home-ways
    Out of their hands, to grasp a star.
Honor to those who are living yet!
    Time shall their laurels make more green!
But at this hour we must not forget
    Those we may call our guests unseen.

One is here whose piercing eyes
    Sharpened young for his country's sake;
Craving more than ambition's prize—
    Great with the plans that brave men make.
Once he saw the flag of the foe
    Mocking a history-hallowed town:
He said, "That banner must be brought low—
    I will go myself and haul it down!"
He climbed the dangerous, giddy stair—
    He braved the ambushes that he passed;
He did not send, but himself went there,
    And stripped the flag from the rebel mast.
His dark eyes flashed in the morning dawn,
    But he fell by a foeman's treacherous crime;
His heart stopped there, but his soul went on,
    And joined the bravest of every clime.
His body sank to untimely rest—
    The glory he sought was snatched away;
But we know that he did his noblest best,
    And gallant Ellsworth is here to-day!

Comes another: so bravely rash,
    And rashly brave, yet steady still;

Turbulent as the thunder's crash,
  But firm as the rocks of an Eastern hill.
And through the valleys and o'er the plain,
  The drum of his horsemen's hoof-beats rolled;
Death knew the pull of his bridle rein,
  And victory gleamed from his locks of gold.
He fought till the Union sky was bright,
  Then flashed his sword in a western sun;
He fell in civilization's fight,
  And died ere half of his days were done.
He camps in the broad blue fields above;
  He needs no laurels upon his brow;
He comes once more for his comrades' love,
  And dashing Custer is with us now!

Another: a silent, mighty soul,
  Who rose from the plane of common things,
To half of the fighting world's control,
  And starred in the list of Triumph's kings.
When humbly toiling for daily bread,
  When soothed by Luxury's rich caress,
When measuring acres of hapless dead,
  Or flushed with the giddy draught, success;
Striving in blood-red clouds of woe
  To lead the land 'neath victory's sun,
Or taking the sword of a fallen foe,
  And writing the great words, "War is done;"
Or ruling the marble halls of state,
  Thrust far to the statesman's utmost goal,
Or ruined by those he found too late
  Were friends of his purse and not his soul;
Or toiling on Mount McGregor's height,
  Longing for days that would let him die,
Waging meanwhile a sturdy fight
  Whenever the foe Despair came nigh;
From earliest life to latest breath,
  Through valleys of woe, o'er hills of pride,
Through glories of life and glooms of death,
  His heart and his brain marched side by side.

The Hudson's shore has his death-stilled heart;
  His hands in that hermit-tomb may rest;
But heroes and graves dwell far apart,
  And Grant to-day is our unseen guest!

Another: a lithe, commanding form,
  Kind features, stern with a soldier-gaze:
A cliff of rock in a battle storm,
  A garden of smiles in peaceful days.
He burned belligerent cities low,
  He planted ruin on every side,
But offered love to a fallen foe,
  And wept when his friend McPherson died.
He shaped his army into a sword,
  And cut the enemy's land in twain,
Yet gave the conquered their kindest word,
  And erred, if ever, to spare them pain.
The office-heroes who fought for place,
  Strove hard to fetter him with their pelf;
But he fought for his country and his race,
  And not for jewels to crown himself.
In times of peace it was his to be
  The foremost gentleman of the land;
Death has no power o'er such as he,
  So reach for the brave old Sherman's hand!

Another: a sturdy Irish heart,
  That gave to this land its life-long aid;
The rush of the whirlwind sped his dart,
  The flash of the lightning fired his blade.
He swore like a trooper, but what he swore
  Was never known to fall or fail;
His oaths in The Book may be blotted o'er,
  For he sinned that God's cause might prevail.
Once freedom's ranks were melting away;
  He moulded panics to victory, then,
Rode down disaster and saved the day;—
  He was good as a hundred thousand men!
His iron heart lies 'neath sods of green,
  His shoulder-stars have been hung away;

But he rides on lofty roads unseen,
    And Sheridan's soul is here to-day!

Another: a tall and sinewy form,
    A face marked deep with the lines of care;
A will of iron, but a heart as warm
    As fiery breeze of the tropic air.
He was born a prince, but in hovels cast—
    He made the cabin a palace, then;
He grew to be more than a king, at last;
    For monarchs, you know, are not always men.
His fight for the crown was hard and grim,
    But his march to the front was firm and true;
He fought for the stars, and the stars for him,
    And God had miracles he must do.
At last he came to his lofty place,
    But wild rebellion was knocking there;
Hot anger frowned at his honest face,
    And desolation was in the air.
He swore that treason should be met
    By every pain that could lay it low,
He rallied ruin against it; yet
    His heart beat warm for every foe.
So on he toiled, till lo! in view
    Swept sacred Emancipation's plan!
He did the deed he was sent to do;
    For God was there, and God knew His man.
Guiding the nation in rocks and shoals,
    He climbed the eternal mast of fame,
And, graced with the thanks of all true souls,
    Wrote Liberator before his name.
His eyes flashed triumph, then swift grew dim—
    A murderer tore that life apart;
But those he loved are still loving him,
    And Lincoln is here in every heart!

But why should I call the muster-roll
    Of those who are here in our hearts to-day?
They need no naming; each true, grand soul
    Has heard your summons and marched this way.

Why call to Hancock, worthy all praise,
  Superb in stature and mental might,
Who helped save Gettysburg's ominous days,
  And left brave blood at that glorious fight?
Why call to Sedgwick—modest man—
  Who longed but to do his duty well;
Who died in the battle's deadly van,
  With no obeisance to shot or shell?
Why call McClellan, whose last life view
  Traced over these hills its eager track,'
Whose soldiers called him their comrade true,
  And spoke of him ever as "Little Mac?"
The Kearneys, the Wadsworths, the Burnsides, the Meades,
  Charge to the front of our memory; they
Endorse their commissions with noble deeds,
  And star in this festal throng to-day.
A mighty and brilliant band is here,
  That none with the eye of flesh may see;
They come from their graves both far and near,
  Their bodies prisoned, their souls set free.
Year after year this unseen throng,
  By death recruited, counts more and more;
And louder and louder the battle-song
  Of heroes that camp on the unseen shore.
If they could speak to us all to-day,
  These words with their greetings would be twined:
"Remember us with what love you may,
  But care for our loved ones left behind.
You give us monuments grand and high,
  You sing to our bravery o'er and o'er,
But let us know that we did not die
  That those we cherished might suffer more!"

And where are the thousands who bravely waged
  A losing strife? Whose hearts were true,
Though false their cause? Whose souls engaged
  Their all in the work they had to do?
The warrior cruelest in the fight,
  Is tenderest to the fallen foe;

"OF HEROES THAT CAMP ON THE UNSEEN SHORE."

The hand that stabs with deadliest might,
  Would stanch forever the crimson flow.
If all of the noblest Southern dead
  Could march together into this place,
With Lee's tall form at the column's head,
  And Stonewall Jackson's calm, kind face,'
And each should bear the smile of a friend,
  As many of those who live have done,
No man that is here, but would straight extend
  The hand of friendship to every one.
The war is over; the strife has fled;
  Love lingers the living ones between;
Let all of the brave Confederate dead
  Be welcomed here as our guests unseen!

The smoke of our cannon has sailed away;
  The clouds are gone and the sky is clear.
Heaven looks from eternal heights to-day,
  And finds that the nation still is here.
The North and the South, the East and West,
  The dead, the living, all agree
That this shall be the grandest—best—
  Of all the nations that time can see;
Shall laugh at centuries as they sweep
  In clouds and sunbeams above its head;
Shall all of our stars in safety keep,
  Shall hold the hands of our patriot dead.
But how? By lying in sloth serene?
  By letting the soldier-spirit cease,
While foreign king and foreign queen
  Still marshal their troops in time of peace?
While hosts of the East march to and fro
  With muskets flashing and bugles that ring,
Ready to grapple with any foe
  With all that discipline's strength can bring?
While navies wander from sea to sea,
  Ready to shell the resistless town,
Able, if conflict with them should be,
  To storm our cities and crush them down?

Rally, O men of the Western land!'
　　You hold this country by heaven's own right!
Strive hard and remember, hand in hand,
　　How best to struggle and how to fight!
God loves sweet peace; but when the laws
　　Of peace are broken by lawless ones,
I notice He loves to have His cause
　　Hedged round with the best of men and guns.
So let us learn in the time of peace
　　The many hardships war may mean,
And never upon our hearts shall cease
　　To glitter the smiles of our guests unseen!

II.

John Jones, of course, made large the day America was born;
He fired a hundred signal-guns to greet the opening morn;
From his cool summer home, a small quaint city 'mongst the isles
That wreathe the broad St. Lawrence' face into its sweetest smiles.
All 'mongst the near Canadian lands the echoes forced their way,
Which sent them back, thus helping much to celebrate the day.

And as the morn with Freedom's sun grew radiant more and more,
A hundred neighbor-islanders came sailing to his shore;
Their tiny frigates decked with flags of patriotic hue,
And faces full of joy and tan, made eloquent the view;
And in a grove where freedom's air was whispering overhead,
When dinners and orations ceased, the following lines were read:

RHYMES TO THE DAY.

Oh, the Fourth of July!
　　When fire-crackers fly,
And urchins in petticoats tyrants defy!
　　When all the still air
　　Creeps away in despair,
And Clamor is king, be the day dark or fair!
　　When Freedom's red flowers
　　Fall in star-spangled showers,
And Liberty capers for twenty-four hours!

When the morn's ushered in
By a sleep-crushing din,
That tempts us to use philological sin!
When the forenoon advances
With large circumstances
Subjecting our lives to debatable chances!
When the soldiers of peace
Their attractions increase,
By marching, protected with clubs of police!
When the little toy-gun
Has its share of the fun,
By teaching short-hand to the favorite son!
When maids do not scream
At the gun's noise and gleam,
Being chock-full of patriotism, gum, and ice-cream!
When horses, hard-bittish,
Get nervous and skittish,
Not knowing their ancestors helped whip the British!
When the family flag,
Full of stars, stripes, and brag,
From the window pops out like a cat from a bag!
When picnic crowds go forth,
Their freedom to throw forth,
Coming back full of patriotism, glory, and so forth!
When long-trained excursions,
With various diversions,
Go out and make work for the doctors and surgeons!
When Uncle Jim Brown
Drives his wagon to town,
Full of gingerbread, children, and thirst—for renown!
When good dear sister Jones
Hears the tumult with groans,
And prays that her children come off with whole bones!
When all fancies and joys
That can compass a noise,
The country in one day of glory employs!
'Tis a glorious time
For a song or a rhyme,
Or a grand cannonade, or an orchestra's chime,

If one can live through it,
And not come to rue it—
The day that our forefathers said they would do it!

Oh, the Fourth of July!
When grand souls hover nigh,
When Washington bends from the honest blue sky!
When Jefferson stands—
Famous scribe of all lands—
The charter of Heaven in his glorified hands!
When his comrade—strong, high
John Adams, comes nigh—
For both went to their rest the same Fourth of July!
When Franklin—grand—droll—
That could lightnings control—
Comes here with his sturdy, progressive old soul!
When Freedom's strong staff,
Hancock—with a laugh—
Writes in Memory's Album his huge autograph!
When old Putnam is met:
Who—they'll never forget—
Showed the foe that a God was in Israel yet!
When Mad Anthony Wayne
Rides up with loose rein,
And receives our encomiums for being insane!
When George the Third, flounced
From this country, well trounced,
Wishes now that his madness had been less pronounced!
When comes Hamilton, fain
To neglect to explain
How so little a form could support such a brain!
When the brave Lafayette,
Our preserver and pet,
Comes again to collect of us Gratitude's debt!
When Marion advances,
(His Christian-name Francis)
Who played for the British in several dances!
When all the souls grand
That made mighty our land,
Around us in hopefulness silently stand,

And wish, beyond doubt,
That they also could shout,
And help ring the anthem of Liberty out!
When the peals of our mirth,
And our claims of true worth,
Are heard to the uttermost ends of the earth;
To the low and the high,
Who the tyrants defy,
A glorious old day is the Fourth of July!

But let thought have its way,
And give memory sway:
Do we think of the cost of this glorified day?
Do we think of the pain
Of the body, heart, brain—
The toils of the living, the blood of the slain?
Should we ever forget
What a deep-mortgaged debt
Has been placed on this date, and exists even yet?
What to our minds saith
The icy cold breath
Of Valley Forge—freezing our soldiers to death?
Can our hearts find a tongue
For those men, old and young,
Who fought while a rope o'er their heads grimly hung?
Of the toils o'er and o'er
That brave Unionists bore,
That our country might not go to pieces once more?
Do we think, while overt
Patriotism we assert,
How a sword-blade will sting—how a bullet can hurt?
Do we feel the fierce strain
Of the edge-belinked chain
That drags through the body—a wounded man's pain?
Do we know, by-the-way,
What it might be to stay
In the wards of a hospital, day after day,
While our life-blood was shed
On a pain-mattressed bed,
And no one we loved to stand near us when dead?

What it may be to lie
'Neath a smoke-blotted sky,
With horse-hoofs to trample us e'en as we die?
Do we think of that boy,
Full of hope, love, and joy,
Who died lest strong men should his country destroy?
Of that husband who fell
In the blood-streaming dell,
Leaving only the memory of battles fought well?
While the harvest field waves,
Do we think of those braves
In the farms quickly planted with thousands of graves?
How the great flag up there,
Clean and pure as the air,
Has been drabbled with blood-drops, and trailed in despair?
Do we know what a land
God hath placed in our hand,
To be made into star-gems, or crushed into sand?
Let us feel that our race,
Doomed to no second place,
Must glitter with triumph or die in disgrace;
That millions unborn,
At night, noon, and morn,
Will thank us with blessings or curse us with scorn,
For raising more high
Freedom's flag to the sky,
Or losing forever the Fourth of July!

III.

But John Jones's hospitality made wide and full display,
Upon that pious carnival yclept Thanksgiving Day;
Which gives more scope to appetite than any other one,
And makes us thankful when at last the feeding all is done.

John Jones, of Philadelphia, on one Thanksgiving tide,
Sent word to every Jones he knew, to hasten to his side;
If rich as Vanderbilt or Gould, or poor as that absurd
Slim biped of the proverb—dear old Job's Thanksgiving bird;

And seated them in padded chairs, wherein they might recline,
When they had dined and dined until they could no longer dine;
And when food's drowsiness began across their nerves to creep,
He read to them the following lines, and put them all to sleep:

THE THURSDAY SABBATH DAY.

It is with us, it is with us, be the weather dark or fair;
See the joy upon the faces, feel the blessings in the air!
Get the dining-chamber ready, let the kitchen fire be filled,
Into gold-leaf slice the pumpkins, have the fatted turkey killed!
Hunt the barn, with hay upholstered, for the ivory-prisoned eggs;
Tie the chickens in a bundle by their strong and yellow legs!
It was eagerly expected, and a year upon its way;
We've a royal welcome ready for the Thursday Sabbath Day!

And we first will go to meeting: where the parson one may hear
Pack in gilded words the blessings that have gathered round the year;
And the choir will sing an anthem full of unincumbered might,
That their stomachs would not let them, if they waited until night;
Older people will sit musing of Thanksgiving mornings fled—
Younger people will sit thinking of Thanksgiving Days ahead;
But they'll join in silent concert when the parson comes to pray,
For the world is all religious on the Thursday Sabbath Day!

Then I hear the kindly racket, and the traffic of old news,
Of a meeting after meeting, 'mid the porches and the pews;
They will tell each other blessings that are fondled o'er and prized—
They will tell each other blessings by Affliction's hand disguised.
For the health that is a fortune, and the harvest full of gold,
Side by side with influenza and rheumatics will be told;
Here we'll hope that many foemen to each other's side may stray:
For the world should all be friendly on the Thursday Sabbath Day!

"Come to dinner!" We are coming, we are coming, fat and spare!
Smell the sweet and savory music of the odors in the air!
Hear the dishes pet each other with their soft and mellow clash!
Feel the snow of loaflets broken, see the table-sabres flash!

Let our palates climb the gamut of delight-producing taste,
Our interiors feel the presence of provisions neatly placed;
Full of thanks and full of praises, full of conversation gay,
Full of everything congenial, on the Thursday Sabbath Day!

Ah, the poor and sick and suffering! To our glad hearts be it known
That God never gave a blessing to be clenched and held alone;
They are brothers, they are sisters, and entitled to their share;
We shall always have them with us—He has put them in our care.
You who clutch at every mercy and devote it to yourselves,
You are putting mammoth treasures on the weakest kind of shelves.
You who take the wares of Heaven and divide them while you may,
Will behold their value doubled, on some other Sabbath Day!

They are coming, they are coming! Let the breezes lisp the tale,
Let the mountains look and see them on the centuries' upward trail;
Let the valleys smile their sweetest, let the lakes their parents greet,
As the river seeks the ocean with its silver-slippered feet.
Let all pleasures be more pleasant, let all griefs with help be nerved;
Let all blessings seek their sources with the thanks that are deserved.
Every spirit must look heavenward, every heart must tribute pay
To the Soul of souls that led us to the Thursday Sabbath Day!

IV.

Jones also celebrated, in a gastronomic way,
That lucky date for humankind he called "Discovery Day;"
He furnished every novel dish that money could command,
Each new discovery how to spoil the works of Nature's hand;
He sent his minions marching through the whole preceding year,
For any new development of cooking quaint and queer.
Each course a revelation was—loud greeted with surprise,
And palatal expectancy, and interested eyes.

And once he turned unto their view a histrionic page:
Annexed unto his dining-room some scenery and a stage;
And when the rich unique dessert its place no longer knew,
The curtain rose, exhibiting a Spanish convent view;

With actors ready to begin a short historic play,
Full of material more or less appropriate to the day.
"These players are new aspirants, whom please do not condemn,"
He murmured to his smiling guests: "'fact, I discovered them."

THREE SCENES IN THE LIFE OF COLUMBUS.[1]

SCENE I., *a hall in the Dominican Convent of Salamanca. Council of learned men assembled to pass judgment on the proposed enterprise of* COLUMBUS. *Enter* TALAVERA, *who calls the Council to order.*

TALAVERA.

Best educated men of all this realm,
Best educated men of all this earth,
Accountants of the past, appraisers of
The present; you who have the trade
Of digging knowledge-nuggets from all times,
And carving them in jewels fit to wear,
Who know what's best and what's best not to know,
Whose learnèd breath upon thought-harvests thrown,
Whips chaff away and leaves the grain of truth:
You have been called together by the King,
Most potent Ferdinand, and by the Queen,
Most pious Isabel, to judge the claims
Of one Columbus; an Italian born,
Who asks of Spain her countenance and help
Through the great Western wilderness of waves,
While he discovers lands to you unknown.

FIRST SCIENTIST.

We need no foreigner to mend our maps.

DEZA.

Soft, learnèd man, let learning teach you patience;
Pass not the judgment till the cause appears.
Let the man speak before you answer him.

TALAVERA.

'Tis well enough. Columbus, state your case;
Unroll your wares; exhibit us a wish.

COLUMBUS (*raising himself proudly*).
I would complete the world!

FIRST SCIENTIST.

                    Irreverent clown!
Pity God did not rest another day,
And let you try your hand!

DEZA.

                    Rest you instead.
Let him enlarge his daring epigram.

COLUMBUS.
So with due modesty and sense I will.   [*Unfolding a chart.*
This world hath leagues that Europe knows not of;
Hath waves that Eastern ship did never cleave;
Hath rivers, forests, islands, continents,
Minds, hearts, and treasures now by distance hidden.
I would sail westward till I find those lands
Where the sun lifts to eastward-gazing eyes;
Would journey still unto the drooping sun,
Through regions of bewildering opulence,
And harvest all for God's own glory—He
Who planted it! I'd give the nation wealth
Greater by far than she has ever wished.
All this I guarantee, if only lent
Strong sails to spread, and crews to man my ships.

TALAVERA.
Here is a Grecian bearing gifts indeed!
Or rather an Italian, offering
To fetch them at our cost. These smooth designs
Brush us with velvet that may cover claws.
Question him, men of learning! Read his mind!

FIRST SCIENTIST.
What university may you be of,
Learnèd philosopher? What your degree?

COLUMBUS.

The ocean is my university;
My sole degree is that of Mariner,
Well tried and always true. Lectures I've heard,
Wherever sailing—'mid the ocean day,
And the dark, treacherous night. The travelled winds
Thundered their lessons at me. I have seen
Many discussions of the deep-voiced waves.
Each star that sees our whole world from the skies
Is a professor to me. I have learned
Much from my own long meditations; whence
A light flames up at last, by which I read
My Heaven-signed commission.

TALAVERA.　　　　　　Well, well, well!
Here is a dreamer!

DEZA.　　　　　Dreams ofttimes come true.

SECOND SCIENTIST.

Nature of course hath schools; men all may read
From alphabets around them; but we hold
All observation naught, until confirmed
By others' words. Tell, then, what hast thou gleaned
From learnèd pens or voices?

COLUMBUS.　　　　　I've conversed
Many a day and night with sea-taught men—
Old sages of the ocean—whose weird tales
Are full of half-hid meaning; they who teach
The classics of the ocean. All the flowers
And weeds of their romances root in truth,
However hidden far may be the soil.
Their tongues have graven these words upon my soul:
THERE'S LAND TO WESTWARD!

THIRD SCIENTIST (*laughing*).
　　　　　　Give him a degree!
Taught by illiterate sailors! Learned man!

3

DEZA.
Still, better than a college-branded fool.

TALAVERA.
Whence is your family, searcher after power?

COLUMBUS.
Though not essential to this argument,
Yet I will answer; it is quickly said:
My father carded wool in Genoa.

FOURTH SCIENTIST.
A prince of sheep-pelts hath come here to pull
The wool across our eyes!

DEZA.
                        Why bring to fore
Questions of birth? 'Tis not so many years,
Your father, herding asses in Castile,
Begot the longest-eared of all his flock.

TALAVERA.
Enough of breeds. Proceed, adventurer.

COLUMBUS.
Call me adventurer then; and so I am,
And so were all accomplishers. No prize
Is won without adventuring. As for birth,
The time will come, when titled families
Will angle for my name, and fight to spread
The lie that I sprang from their mouldy roots.
My deeds be my escutcheon!

TALAVERA.   Cease your boasts,
And give performances—at least, in words.

COLUMBUS.
From all that I have learned—seen—meditated—
All I have viewed with Inspiration's help,

From every hill of thought God leads me to,
I swear that on the farther side o' the earth,
Balancing that which we now know and walk,
Is land!—great continents of unknown land!
Which I can reach, with westward-pointed prow,
And through it Asia, with her wealth-crammed mines,
All to be thus for God's own glory gained.

DEZA.
Bravo!—thrice bravo!—'tis a mingled voice
Of Heaven and Earth, that brings these words to us!

FIFTH SCIENTIST.
All hail to this discoverer of new lands—
This king of topsy-turvey, whose domains
Cling unto earth as do the barnacles
Sometimes upon the bottom of a ship!
Stand him upon his head and crown his heels!
Despatch him for his realms in ships capsized!
He shall send word of matters in his land,
In characters inverted; he shall tell
How rain falls upward; how the forest trees
Tower downward in the cellarage of space;
His subjects, taking lessons from the flies,
Shall creep along earth's ceiling dextrously,
Lest they might fall and strike against a star;
He shall write, " Have you any medicines
For rush of blood to th' head? If so, please send
Them quickly as you can!"

DEZA.
                        If so there be
Medicaments that maybe might induce
A rush of brains to th' head, send you for them.

COLUMBUS.
This world's a miracle, made by our God—
Himself Great Miracle of Miracles.
All things are relative; and it may be

That they who stand upon Earth's other rim
Look downward as do we.

SIXTH SCIENTIST.

His head is turned.
But, mystic mariner, suppose you reach
Those far-off countries: how will you bring back
The ships and treasures that you took from us,
To say nought of the riches that you find?
How would you contract for a western gale
So strong that it will push you up the hill
That you have glided o'er so easily?*

SEVENTH SCIENTIST.
More miracles The whole thing shall be done
By miracle!

EIGHTH SCIENTIST.

Since **God's** hand is besought
To help this project, it perchance were well
To ask Him His opinion of the same.
I have here fifty texts from sacred books,
Proving this scheme to be illusory,
Which, so it please the Council, I will read.

DEZA.
Block not this pious project with the Bible!
Do you not know that in its mystery-depths
Are pearls whose gleam our weak eyes cannot see?

COLUMBUS.
Little by little, as **God** gives us light,
We read the sacred cipher of His word;
Not only of His word, but of His works,
Doth He reveal Himself. He would have us
To know and do and conquer for ourselves.

---

* Strange as it may now appear, these, and many other equally brilliant arguments,
were advanced against Columbus' scheme by the so-called learned men of the time.

Though Science and Religion long may frown
And flout each other coldly—neither one
The other understanding—time may be
When they can dwell together. Then will come
Their wedding-day, and the world shall rejoice.

TALAVERA.
You should be pious—you who prophesy
So glibly of heaven-work. But what hear I
Of various indiscretions your wild soul
Has not escaped? Inform us fully, seer.

COLUMBUS (*hanging his head*).
I am not perfect. I have borne grave sins
That plague me sore. The very monk is here
To whom I have confessed.

DEZA.   This Council, then,
Is a confessional, which seeks perfection?
Perfection then should rule it. Let him rise,
Whose morals have no flaw—who in his heart
(Which, we are told, can nothing hide from God)
Hath ne'er committed sin. If any one
Who'll stand my cross-examination for an hour
Be here, pray let him rise and quiz this man,
And summon Heaven to witness what he says.
            [*A strange and sudden interval of silence.*

FIRST SCIENTIST.
            I have friends that I must meet,
            Waiting me in yonder street.   [*Exit.*

SECOND SCIENTIST.
            I must go and con a book
            In yon cloister's quiet nook.   [*Exit.*

THIRD SCIENTIST.
            Leaving quickly I must be,
            As my dinner waits for me.   [*Exit.*

FOURTH SCIENTIST.

> I a map **must** finish soon,
> Of the mountains of the moon.

　　　　　　　　　　　　　　　　[*Exit.*

FIFTH SCIENTIST.

> I must teach a class of youth
> First-class cosmographic truth.　　[*Exit.*
> 　　　　[*The Council breaks up in confusion.*

————　·

SCENE II., *Court of Barcelona.* COLUMBUS, *having returned from his successful and triumphant voyage, is enjoying a grand reception by the delighted monarchs,* ISABELLA *and* FERDINAND. *They seat him beside them.*

FERDINAND.

> Grandest sailor of the zones,
> 　Piercer of the storm-cloud's breast,
> Finder of the lost unknowns,
> 　Joiner of the East and West,
> Julius Cæsar sent from Spain,
> 　Conqueror of the setting sun,
> Alexander of the main,
> 　All the heroes fused in one,
> Thou perchance hast made our lot
> Regions such as Rome had not;
> Thou wilt bring us splendors grand,
> Such as Spain has never seen;
> Thou wilt make our twofold land
> Of this earth the treasurer-queen.
> Thou, the king of storm and tide,
> Now art welcome at our side;
> Thou art worthy in the gleam
> Of our jewelled crowns to beam;
> Welcome to these hearts and hands,
> Admiral of the Western lands!

　　　　　　　　　　　[*Te Deum Laudamus*

ISABELLA.

> Music not on earth is met,
> Word hath not been written yet,

"GRANDEST SAILOR OF THE ZONES."

Splendor cannot breed display
Worthy of God's praise to-day!
Nothing mind or heart can raise
Are sufficient for his praise.
He hath led our messenger,
Unappalled by mortal fear,
Through the forests of the waves,
Over luckless seamen's graves;
Climbing, on his mission strange,
Many an ocean mountain range,
Till he touched th' uncharted strand
Of a wealth-strewn pagan land.
'Mong new millions, that ne'er heard
Preaching of the Sacred Word,
He hath given us the glory
First to bear the Sacred Story;
Richest honors now confer
On this brave-souled messenger!

COLUMBUS.
Sovereigns of the twofold reign,
Rulers of my heart and brain—

INSANE WOMAN (*rushing into presence of sovereigns*).
Give me my husband back! Give him to me, I say!
What do I care for his worlds? He took my world away!
What is your praise to Heaven, while Heaven your cruelty grieves?
I want my husband back! Give him to me, you thieves!
Oh, shake your diamond robes, dazzle my eyes as you may!
Crown this foreigner-villain that takes our husbands away!
Yes, he has brought you gold, robbed from good men's lives;
Yes, he has brought you Indians, stolen from others' wives;
Ingrate! where is the woman who loved and cherished you?[6]
Why do you keep to yourself the part that is her due?

> [*She is dragged away by the guards, still struggling
> and screaming.*

COLUMBUS.
Sovereigns of the twofold reign,
Rulers of my heart and brain,

Dear these honors are to me,
 Sweeter, for the toil and danger,
 Than I found—unwelcome stranger—
On the wide, mysterious sea.
Mariners of royal life,
You who sailed the waves of strife;
You who pressed the camp's rough pillows,
You who breasted war's red billows,
For the meed of sacred fame,
And Christ's holy sacred name,
Now in heathen lands His wraith
 In that sepulchre still lies,'
'Mid those hordes of pagan faith.
 Sad and suffering are His eyes,
Drooping are His nail-scarred hands;
Can you hear His mild commands?
Can you hear His sacred moans?
" I am not among my own ;
They received me not when living,
 They protect me not when dead.
Must I suffer—still forgiving—
 In a foeman-guarded bed?"
Sovereigns, I the vow have made
 That this Western march of mine
Shall be first of a crusade
 To that Eastern tomb divine.
When, through walls of darkest night,
First I saw that signal-light,
When, at far approach of day,
Ere the starlight sailed away,
There amid the twilight grand
Loomed the longed-for prize of land—

  [*Enter* RODRIGO DE TRIANA, *a mariner, struggling*
   through the guards.

RODRIGO.
Give me my velvet doublet, and my pension!'

FERDINAND.
Hush, mariner! your tongue makes scars within
Our solemn festival.

RODRIGO.   No wonder, king!
This Christ you fight for, did not He denounce
Injustice? Shall this Christless Christian, then,
Pose in His name? 'Twas I who first found land!
He saw a light, he says, in the black west.
Is fire, then, land? Or, "'twas a fisherman,
Whose torch arose and fell upon the waves!"
Is a boat land? Boats are for lack of land.
If boats are land, we carried land with us.
Or who can tell what boat the light was of?
Perchance some other member of our fleet.
Why should, then, this white-polled Italian rogue—
Laden from hold to deck with honors—try
To steal a sailor's hammock? Say I still,
Give me my velvet doublet and my pension!

FERDINAND.
How's this, Columbus?

COLUMBUS.   Nothing care I, King,
For doublet or for pension; only still
To hold the honor first t' have sighted land.

ISABELLA.
But one admitted, they must go together.

COLUMBUS (*firmly*).
Then I claim all.—

RODRIGO.
                 And lose your lie-gashed soul.—
Forger of log-books—swindler of your crews—
Wear on your crest an honest sailor's curse!
May all your glory rust to iron chains
That drag you through disgrace! I pray to God
That when I found those isles, I found your grave!
May others steal your credit and your fame!
May e'en your name be blotted from that land
You claim you have discovered!"

FERDINAND.   Guards, he raves;
Tear him away.

RODRIGO (*struggling as he is borne along*).
          I'll to another land,
And try Mahomet's justice. Farewell, thief!

COLUMBUS.
Perchance he knows where still are other worlds,
And can lead other sailors there, as I
Led him to that.

ISABELLA.
               Mind not these summer clouds
That flit before your glory. You shall now
Give us in detail all that you have seen
In yonder land of wonders. Who comes here?

          [*Enter* FIRST, SECOND, THIRD, FOURTH, FIFTH, SIXTH.
          and SEVENTH SCIENTISTS.[19]

FIRST SCIENTIST.
          Grand Confirmer of my views,
          Welcome, with thy dazzling news!

SECOND SCIENTIST.
          Learning's true and valiant knight,
          Well I knew that thou wast right!

THIRD SCIENTIST.
          All opposing voice be stilled!
          My predictions are fulfilled!

FOURTH SCIENTIST.
          Heaven in mercy hath devised
          That my hopes be realized!

FIFTH SCIENTIST.
          Brother of our learnèd band,
          Let me shake thy hardy hand!

SIXTH SCIENTIST.

> What can courage not display,
> When we scholars lead the way?

SEVENTH SCIENTIST.

> Tracer of our well-mapped sea,
> We must give you a degree!

DEZA.

> Scholars, call him, if you please,
> Brave Bewilderer of Degrees,
> Grand Extinguisher of Schools,
> Taught by educated fools;
> Give Columbus this degree:
> Famous Foe of Pedantry.

SCENE III., *a humble room in the city of Valladolid.* COLUMBUS *dying. He speaks to his servant.*

Lift me down softly—softly!—this crushed form
Is dying old—old even beyond its years.
Is this my prayer-book? I have grown half-blind,
Hunting for worlds. Now once more must I search
And find my future home, where, maybe, I
Can serve beneath a king who will be just.
My breath drags anchor.—Ah! and so the Queen
Has abdicated for a higher throne,
And sleeps on beds of marble. I would fain
Have kissed once more that warm and shapely hand,
And drank again her blue eyes' sympathy,
And felt the heart-help of her soft, sweet voice.
Christ grant we heav'n together! Paradise
Would be a lonely port without my Queen.
Ah, Pain! Pain! Pain! how you are mocking me!
Is 't what I have done brings these agonies,
Or good left undone? Yes, I've much of both
T' account for; but my steps meant to be true.

Ah! 'twas a glorious dream—that grand crusade
Westward—to win Christ's Empire in the East!
Th' accomplishing of it might have been enough
T' have saved me now from dying poor—alone—
Nor son nor brother near me. 'Tis my fate;
Whatever Christ ordains—that be my fate;
It may be 'tis for needful discipline:
All purgatories are not after death.

Ah, that October morning! 'Twas a life—
'Twas twenty—fifty—nay, a thousand lives
Of days and nights eventless—when, behold,
My first land smiled upon me from the West!
It was a fairy dream come over-true;
It was a score of prostrate, plodding years
Turned upright toward the skies! It was my word
Shown to be gold 'mong the black dust of scorn
That covered it for tedious nights and days!
"Land! Land! Land! Land!" the happy sailors cried ·
"You are a god!" they shouted: "You tore down
The key to Heaven's far secret! You are blessed
By all the saints!" They crawled and kissed my feet;
They begged for favors in my new domains;
They prayed for pardons of past mutinies;
But all that was as nothing. Came a voice,
Out of some unknown regions of my soul:
"You have found fame that ne'er can be forgot!
You are the greatest conqueror history knows!
A new, grand kind of conqueror—one who finds
The lands he subjugates!"—My God! my God!
Will nothing still this pain? It murders me!

Then my return! That bright land-voyage from
Seville to Barcelona! Surging waves
Of loud applause broke swiftly o'er my bark,
And gales of acclamation swept me on.
No more I tossed in Poverty's canoe;
My land-cruise was a fleet of brigantines,
With Victory's flag far flowing from the mast!

Ah, that rich April day, when the brave Queen
At Barcelona drew me to her throne!
When the wool-comber's tardily-honored son
Rode, king-like, through the flag-trimmed, shouting streets,
Escorted by Spain's grandest cavaliers,
Wherein proud generations stored their blood—
Whereon a thousand victory-jewels gleamed!
That was a life—a thousand lives in one!
My painted Indians walked along the street,
Like prisoners in a Roman triumph. Though
Some tears they shed, brewed by their home-sick hearts,
Some sighs they wafted toward the dreamy West,
Some pangs they suffered for their absent loves;
'Twas but required to heap my glory full;
My triumph's throne must needs foundation find
On some one's woe (all earthly honors crush
Beneath their feet the hopes of some who fail);
Women raved at me for their husbands, dead;
(All victories flaunt their banners over graves!)
Old Rodrigo deemed he discovered first
The land I brought him to:—well, every prize
Is grudged by those who lose it. 'Twas too sad
To see the poor, sour, disappointed man
Dive to the depths of infidelity!
Better, perhaps, t' have given him the boon,
Than see him lose that greatest boon—his soul!

My second voyage! That September morn
I sailed from Cadiz! No more humbleness!
How they all fawned upon me! "Here he comes!"
The great Columbus! Ah, no one like me!
I was an angel! (One, be't understood,
That could endure all hardships for their sakes,
An angel with earth-favors he could grant.)
I walked among the cringing, common clay,
An Alexander without stature's lack,
For I towered head and shoulders 'bove them all!
How like a sailor-king I looked and felt!
'Twas a great day! And even then there came

(As always may—a cloud to every sky)
A bent and withered crone close to my side,
And whispered shrilly upward in my ear:
"Give credit to the pilot and his crew
Who lent you log and charts at Tercerns;
Then died within your house and told no tales!'"
I pushed the hag away, but not the lie:
It clung to me, and formed a dingy stain
On my renown, and always will be told.
Heaven rest the poor old pilot; I even had
To lend him charts with which to seek for heaven!
How little did he think to mar my fame!

Ah, that sad voyage homeward, decked in chains!
When Bobadilla—proud, religious knave—
Judge and attorney both—condemning me
From his ship's deck—before he reached my land!
Then, Espinosa—menial, scullion, slave—
A creature I had lifted from sad depths—
Hammered the fetters on my storm-scarred wrists.
So, with such jewels, I re-entered Spain;
So different from the glory-spangled day
When I brought back an empire in my hands!
The golden age of my career!—and this—
The grim iron age; yet no less proud was I,
Bearing sore envy's heavy metal gibes,
Than its unwilling plaudits.

        Then those years
Through which I tarried to have justice done;
Nor lingered in the anteroom of sloth
(Waiting, with idleness, breeds agony),
But sailed for other crowns to give my Queen.
Even my old age toiled for this land of Spain
(Adopted by me—rich-brained foreigner—
And left a legacy of priceless worth)
As faithful as my prime. Oh, how they surge
And dash against my memory's dreary shore—
Those days and nights of age-resisted toil!
Days that I should have passed in glorious ease,

Nights that I should have slept on silken beds,
Surrounded by the splendors I had earned.

And here I die, attended by no crowd
Of waiting messengers, to tell the world
That it has lost a hero. Well, 'tis well!
I perish here as poor as I was born;
But so do all. The grave is Death's frontier,
Impassable; and even if 'twere not,
The living seize the wealth of th' dying ones.
A worthless, poor old mariner I die;
And so do all; launching on unknown seas,
And landing where—they can but only hope.
With all earth's living heroes far from me,
I die; and still cannot forego to think
That great discoveries may make glad this voyage,
Of such as each soul must make for itself;
That all the sailors of that farther shore
Will meet me when I land, and hail me chief.   [*He dies.*

[*Enter the spirits of* FREEDOM *and* PROGRESS.

SPIRIT OF FREEDOM.

    Thou who foundst the free-born West,
    Enter, strong, free soul, to rest.
    Thou hast opened wide the door
    Into refuge evermore,
    Of those who, with longings high,
    Cringe beneath an eastern sky.
    Thou shalt always honored be,
    By the Empire of the Free:
    By that land across the main,
    Which will far out-dazzle Spain;
    Which, within the centuries bright,
    That shall follow these of night,
    Will disperse its beams afar,
    As sometimes the morning-star
    Sheds an earth-detected ray
    In the glaring Summer day.
    Rest, thou search-light of the sea,
    Homeward thou didst guide the free!

SPIRIT OF PROGRESS.

Hero, rest, but not for long:
All the brave and true and strong
Who possess the Hidden Land,
Soon will come to press thy hand.
Thou hadst flaws: thy gleaming brain
Bore some rust from Error's chain;
Thy fault-flecked but generous heart
From earth-passions could not part;
But if ever pain and grief
Out of glory snatched relief,
If the quarried gold can shine
When uncovered in the mine,
If the darkness can take flight
When appears the morning light,
All thy woes shall be redressed,
Patient Finder of the West;
All thy earth-born faults condoned,
Though by cavillers bemoaned;
Thy wrongs shall be made a theme
   Of the true historian's choice,
And the poet's waking dream,
   And the marble's silent voice.
When that late-born western land
Shall be rich and great and grand,
It will show its treasures vast—
   It will celebrate its fame—
With a pageant unsurpassed—
   Bearing thy illustrious name."
Long as Humankind believe
That 'tis duty to achieve;
Long as Faith can struggle free
For what she cannot yet see;
Long as Toil aspires to gain
Glory from fatigue and pain;
Long as Earth keeps on its way,
Marching, marching every day,
THE COLUMBUS still shall not
Be neglected or forgot.

FESTIVAL OF THE JOLLY CLERGYMEN.

Festival of the Jolly Clergymen.

THEY met on Saturday, its night—
    A jolly club of prosperous preachers—
Who knew that merriment was right,
    In all its non-abhorrent features;
Who did not think one's meed of grace
Depended on his length of face;
Who laughed and wept with swinging rhymes,
And talked of merry, rough old times;
And roasted many a queer lay-brother,
And cracked sly jokelets on each other;
In short, did everything inside
A proper ministerial pride,
To get them into fluent vein,
And rest them for the Sunday strain.

One night, half silently, these men
    The past and present were comparing;
Mused how much better now than then,
    The couriers of the Lord were faring;
How large the salary and the fee,
Compared to what they used to be;
How far their present clothes surpassed
The ones they long aside had cast;
How much more freely bread-and-meat
Exposed itself for them to eat;
How rich to-day their church-bells' chimes,
Compared to those of olden times;
This, with no vanity of head,
But thankfulness of heart instead.

And oft they thought of precious hours:
    The calms they'd fought, the tempests weathered:
While in their hearts they'd pressed the flowers
    In country wastes and gardens gathered;
And some who had not known the joy
Of being in humble folks' employ,
And had not had the discipline
Of those who destitute had been,
Themselves were happy to avail
Of many a heart-instructive tale,
With listening ears and honest eyes,
And power to deeply sympathize;
In short, this Club's doors did not pass
A single ministerial ass.

And oft they thought of those who now
    Within unstreeted fields were striving,
With yearning heart and aching brow,
    And pay that scarce involved surviving;
Of those who press the bloody sands
And jungled fields of heathen lands;
Of those whose work is worldly-drear,
Upon the thorny-ground frontier;
Of those whom age and helplessness
Have thrown in idle-houred distress;
Of those who toil in places low
As some where Christ was wont to go;
Ere ceased this subject to prevail,
A brother told the following tale:

ELDER LAMB'S DONATION.

Good old Elder Lamb had labored for a thousand nights and days,
And had preached the blessèd Gospel in a multitude of ways;
Had received a message daily over Faith's celestial wire,
And had kept his little chapel full of flames of heavenly fire;
He had raised a numerous family, straight and sturdy as he could,
And his boys were all considered most unnaturally good;

And his slender salary kept him, till went forth the proclamation,
" Let us pay him up, this season, with a generous, large donation."

So they brought him hay, and barley, and some corn upon the ear.
Also straw enough to bed a livery-stable for a year;
And they strewed him with potatoes of inconsequential size,
And some onions, whose completeness drew the moisture to his eyes;
And some cider—more like water, in an inventory strict—
And some apples, pears, and peaches, that the autumn gales had
    picked;
And some strings of dried-up apples—mummies of the fruit crea-
    tion—
Went to swell the doleful chorus of old Elder Lamb's donation.

Also radishes and turnips pressed the pumpkin's cheerful cheek;
Likewise, beans enough to furnish half of Boston for a week;
And some eggs, whose inner nature bore the legend, " Long ago,"
And some butter that was worthy to have Samson for a foe;
And some stove-wood, green and crooked, on his flower-beds was
    laid,
Fit to furnish fire departments with the most substantial aid.
All things unappreciated found this night their true vocation,
In that great museum of relics, known as Elder Lamb's donation.

There were biscuits whose material was their own secure defence;
There were sauces whose acuteness bore the sad pluperfect tense;
There were jellies quaintly flavored, there were mystery-laden pies;
There was bread that long had waited for the signal to arise;
There were cookies, tasting clearly of the dim and misty past;
There were doughnuts that in justice 'mongst the metals might be
    classed;
There were chickens, geese, and turkeys, that had long been on pro-
    bation,
Now received in full connection, at old Elder Lamb's donation!

Then they brought his wife a wrapper, made for some one not so tall.
And they gave him twenty slippers, every one of which was small;
And they covered him with sackcloth, as it were, in various bits,
And they clothed his helpless children in a wardrobe of misfits.

And they trimmed his house with "Welcome!" and some bric-à-brac-
    ish trash—
And one absent-minded brother brought five dollars, all in cash!
Which the good old pastor handled with a thrill of exultation,
Wishing that in filthy lucre might have come his whole donation!

Morning broke at last in splendor; but the Elder, bowed in gloom,
Knelt amid decaying produce and the ruins of his home.
But his piety had never till that morning shone so bright,
For he prayed for those who'd brought him to that unexpected plight;
But some worldly thoughts intruded: for he wondered, o'er and o'er,
If they'd buy that day at auction what they gave the night before.
And his fervent prayer concluded with the natural exclamation,
"Take me to Thyself in grace, O Lord, before my next donation!"

————

And once, the conversation's scope
    Took in those pastors who, desiring
To do more than they ought to hope,
    Were less effective than aspiring;
Whose plans so loomed and roared and glared,
With their ability compared,
As to remain in dust and doubt,
Unable to be carried out.—
Illustrating, with much thought-gain,
Religious matters with profane,
And seeing the fact, through great and small,
That all things may resemble all,
A clergyman, sedate and old,
The following short, true story told:

McFLUFFEY'S CANOE.

My boatman laughed loud at a man on the shore,
With habiliments proud and assurance galore,
And a manner that sought the idea to convey,
That he maybe had bought the whole river that day:
Said my shrewd Irish lad, as a droll glance he threw,
"He remoinds me, bedad, of McFluffey's canoe.

"' TAKE ME TO THYSELF IN GRACE, O LORD, BEFORE MY NEXT DONATION !' "

"Oh, McFluffey was 'there' in compethitive sail:
He could show his back hair in the calm or the gale;
He was absent upon any shpot but firrst place,
Till he enthered the John J. O'Flanigan race:
Which it tore him all down, an' then shwept him up, too,
Wid some frinds, who now frown on McFluffey's canoe.

"For he'd said, 'Oi'll hew out a new craft, loike as not,
That 'll prance all about every craft yez have got;
An' her patthern Oi'll kape to mesilf—good or bad—
For the crayture Oi'll shape in me cellar, bedad;
Oi'll be makher, desoigner, an' captain an' crew—
There'll not be a foiner 'n McFluffey's canoe.'

"So this promisin' craft in his cellar he shaped,
An' he chuckled and laughed, an' he pounded and schraped;
An' his dhry dock was wet wid the shmell of ould gin,
But we never could get us a pull to go in.
An' he says, 'Cork yer eyes till the proper toime, you,
An' ye'll have a surprise wid McFluffey's canoe!'

"An' the race-day did lind a fair breeze an' broight sun,
An' we backed our ould frind about twinty to one;
An' we pitied the fate of the others afloat,
An' shouted, 'Just wait for McFluffey's new boat!'
An' he says, 'She's as staunch as me frinds are, an' true;
So shtep down an' hilp launch ould McFluffey's canoe!'

"An' we shouted, 'All right!' an' went down wid glad grin,
An' we pushed our sails tight wid a pull at the gin;
An' the boat shtood there fresh, all as shwate as could be;
Oh, a first-class professional beauty was she!
An' his shwatcheart had sewed a green flag, trimmed wid blue.
An' her name had bestowed on McFluffey's canoe!

"An' we lifted her clane on our shoulders, in pairs—
The boat, sure, I mane—and descended up-stairs;
But the boat was too great, sure—the door was too shmall—
We couldn't get the crayture evicted, at all!

Not a door could be shlammed that the chraft would sail through,
An' we shtood there becalmed with McFluffey's canoe!

"'Saw the floor! smash the wall! blow the roof off!' he cried:
But nothing at all would admit her outside;
An' Mac swelled up in girth, an' blasphamed himsilf sick,
An' then prayed for an earthquake to come, an' be quick!
Shtone an' brick would not moind it, whate'er we moight do;
An' the race lift behoind it McFluffey's canoe!

"An' his shwateheart the shock drove wid rage most insane.
An' she shtamped through the dock, when he thried to explain;
An' she said, 'Look-a-there!' wid the rage in her face,
'The *Bridget O'Flaherty's* winnin' my race!
You decaivin' ould elf!' an' her words fairly flew;
'Now be off wid yerself, an' yer dirthy canoe!'

"Now whin a man brings me a high-moighty sound
Concernin' some things *he* is goin' to bring round,
An' thanks his good stars *he* is winnin' the day,
Forgettin' the bars that men find in their way,
I says, wid sly laughter, 'Yer pride yez may rue:
Yer a-modellin' afther McFluffey's canoe!'

"An' when a man linds all his plans to himself,
An' lays all his frinds for a while on the shelf,
An' thinks he knows twice what there is to be known,
An' the outside advice will be lettin' alone,
I says, 'If yer pride to a point yez don't hew,
Ye'll be takin' a ride in McFluffey's canoe!'"

———

And soon the Club were blithe of tongue,
 With marital congratulation,
For one of them, who'd lately sprung
 Into a bridegroom's happy station;
And various nuggets of advice
Were coined in precepts smooth and nice;

And now and then a warning word
From sages celibate was heard;
And several instances were cited
Where those who had been so united,
Had lived together very well
(As if 'twere something strange to tell);
And one good brother amplified
This story of a pastor's bride:

ELDER PETTIGREW'S HELPMEET.

Elder Pettigrew was married on the fifteenth of July,
And some sixteen jealous maidens let their disappointment fly;
And some seventeen other maidens scorned to give their sorrow air,
And some eighteen other maidens laughed, and said they didn't care;
And some nineteen other maidens felt the fact come rather near,
For the Elder's face was handsome, and his heart was full of cheer.

And his older friends were sorry he had done as he had done,
For the bride was young and little, and retiring as a nun;
To be sure, her face was comely; still, she wasn't much to see,
And they had their own opinion what a pastor's bride should be.
And they said, "Lone-handed pastors ought to search, and search, and
    search,
Till they get a proper partner that can help them run the church."

And she closed her eyes devoutly, or looked down upon the floor,
When the fateful fact was mentioned that her maiden days were o'er;
And her voice was just a flutter, and her answering timid-low;
Even her would-be rivals pitied, that she had to tremble so;
But when once the fact was stated that she was the pastor's wife,
She glanced round upon the people, with a newish lease of life.

And the next day in the morning, from her new-found social perch
She began to help the preacher to reorganize the church;
For she called upon the sisters, with a look of brooding care,
And reformed the sewing-circle into quite a new affair;
And she called upon the Deacons, with a smile that never ceased,
And requested that the salary of her husband be increased;

And she never missed an effort, till she laid the old choir waste,
And discharged the ones whose voices did not satisfy her taste;
And she straightway formed a new one, full of singers of her choice,
And became herself the leader, more by gesture than by voice;
And permitted no flirtations at such times when she was nigh,
For she held them all in bondage by the glimmer of her eye;

And the Sunday-school and missions glided under her control,
And she made investigation of the state of every soul;
And the charities were also reconstructed by her hand,
No withholding ever prospering, that evaded her command;
And the rich were asked assistance for the causes of her choosing,
In a manner that they somehow had no method of refusing;

And the sermons got to sounding (or, by Fancy's logic bid,
Several of the congregation thought they knew they thought they did),
Quite as if they were constructed on a new and fem'nine plan,
And a stern appeal for Woman, as against the tyrant Man.
And the folks looked at each other, with their faces new-forlorn,
Whispering low, "She writes his sermons, just as sure as you are
    born!"

And one day her husband's larynx was not wholly in repair,
And she coolly took the pulpit, with a firmly modest air;
And proceeding with a sermon, with determined look, though sad,
She discoursed a great deal better than her husband ever had.
Then the people looked and wondered, and inquired, "What shall we
    do?
For the one that gets no salary, is the smarter of the two!"

Till at last, one day, the places that had known her ceased to know,
And the parsonage was darkened, and the people whispered low.
There had come a wailing couple from The Land where All Begins.
And their naming was elaborate, but the people called them "Twins;"
And the lady abdicated from her sacerdotal throne,
And suggested to her husband that he run the church alone.

And amid the smiles and sorrows of the following twenty years,
Came some fifteen other children to the land of smiles and tears;

"AND ONE DAY HER HUSBAND'S LARYNX WAS NOT WHOLLY IN REPAIR."

And the manse's mistress gave up all her managerial goals,
And devoted strict attention to her children's precious souls;
And remarked to wondering neighbors, not to be misunderstood,
"She who starts her children heavenward, works as God desires she
    should."

And her sons proved mostly preachers, shedding goodness all their
    lives,
And her daughters "joined the movement" by becoming preachers'
    wives;
And though not the brightest day-star that his Conference ever knew,
Never-ceasing good resulted, thus, from Elder Pettigrew;
And the modest little woman (leastways, everybody said it)
Was entitled to some ninety-nine one-hundredths of the credit.

They closed at midnight with a song
    From Rev. Thomas Thompson Thomas,
Whose voice was sweet, as well as strong,
    With well developed mines of promise;
Whose tones could make the rafters ring,
And coax the walls themselves to sing;
Elicit sympathetic tears,
Or fill the room with laughs and cheers;
Whose manner had magnetic thrills
That fashioned nerves unto their wills;
Whose heart, while touring with his voice,
Made others suffer or rejoice;
So, while the clock for midnight rang,
The singing preacher sweetly sang:

HYMN-SERMON.

Text: "Safely through another week."

Seven days' dangers passed us by:
Perils strewn from earth to sky;
Clouds within whose chambers deep
Fire and flood together sleep;

Air in ambush, which, set free,
Might a cyclone-panther be;
Earthquakes in the realms below,
Prowling fiercely to and fro;
Sickness that, with stealthy tread,
Brought the grave its hapless dead;
So the words in song we speak:
"Safely through another week."

Who could sail without the waves?
   Who could breathe without the air?
Men were only walking graves—
   But that God is everywhere.
Stars that travel, fast or slow,
   Through the countries of the sky,
On His errands come and go—
   With His viewless wings they fly.
Each true spirit is a star
   Fed by one Eternal Ray;
So the words we sing afar:
   "God has brought us on our way."

Lo the diamond—metal sun!
And by toil and pain 'twas won.
Learning comes the world to bless—
It was purchased with distress.
See a fame in glory rise!
It was bought with sacrifice.
Feel a love that passeth thought!
But it did not come unbought.
With exertion and desire,
Souls must clamber and aspire;
So we sing, in accents meek:
"Let us all a blessing seek."

Did you view the morning rise?
   To the eye a wondrous feast!
Precious stones bestrewed the skies—
   Heaven's own gate hung in the east.

Can you see the mountains grand?
  Do you hear the robin sing?
Worship, O my soul! you stand
  In a palace of the King!
Splendor lurks in every spot
  Of this Sabbath morn's display:
Fellow-singers, are we not
  "Waiting in His courts to-day?"

You whose life-webs weigh like lead,
Weave to-day a golden thread;
You who bend 'neath labor's rod,
Bow this day to none but God;
You who toil for Learning's goal,
Read to-day your child's sweet soul;
You whose heart is doomed to bear
Sorrow, shame, and needless care.
Come, to-day, and lay them prone
On the white steps of the Throne.
Properly is this confessed:
"Day of all the week the best."

Do not lie in slumber's thrall,
  You who would with heaven rise;
Do not let 'midst rubbish fall
  This gold ladder to the skies.
You must join the child-like throng
  Yearning for a Father's love;
You must help to make the song
  That is waited for above.
Toil, that others you may see
  By the powers of goodness blessed;
Then your Sunday-life will be
  "Emblem of Eternal Rest."

A FESTIVAL OF THE SKY CLUB.

A Festival of the Sky Club.

THE Sky Club was a small association
Of men retired from lofty navigation,
To join which none need cultivate pretensions,
Who had not made at least thirteen ascensions.

This club, who, half their lives, with clouds were floating.
And through air-waves had, so to speak, been boating,
Now crawled about, with hands and feet to aid them,
As Nature meant, when wingless first she made them.
One had one good arm, but it was the only;
Another's leg had many years walked lonely;
And almost all bore some eraseless markings
Attendant on aerial disembarkings.

The emblems of this club were simple, very,
And made unthinking minds unduly merry:
A rooster, sheep, and duck, of lofty manners,
Comprised the heraldry upon their banners
(The first-named animals that history mentions
That were addicted to balloon ascensions,
Before men made of fear so great a stranger
That they themselves incurred aerial danger);
Their walls bore prints of men of every nation
Who'd overcome the curse of gravitation:
Of Dædalus, ingenious artist-Grecian—
Who made him wings, with wax their sole cohesion;
Escaped Crete's monarch's rage-compounded virus,
And flew to Sicily (upon papyrus);

5

Of Icarus, his son, who started nicely
Equipped, it seems, with similar wings precisely;
But making, for ambition or diversion,
A sunward trip—a little branch excursion—
Found that the sun of wing-wax was a melter,
And dropped into the ocean, helter-skelter;
Of old Archytas, who made, with much trying,
A pigeon out of wood, and set it flying
(Which should have less in webs of wonder wound us,
Than genuine live ones floating all around us);
Of Roger Bacon, who by book suggested
That lofty navigation should be tested;
Thought we could sail, with proper means and motion,
Top of the air, the same as of the ocean;
And, daring sceptic earth-worms to deny it,
Was sagely anxious some one else should try it;
Of those French aeronauts, Montgolfier Brothers,
Who also left their goings up to others;

But over these, and twice as large, were staring
Rozier and Arlandes, who, with NEW daring,
In the hushed sight of curious, breathless legions,
First travelled up to hyper-mundane regions;
And Blanchard, who scored sixty good ascensions,
Then died in bed, with purse of poor pretensions;
Of Mrs. B., his wife, who, metal-sinewed,
Her husband's business at th' old stand continued:
Fired rockets off while in the air suspended,
Caught fire herself, and like a stick descended;
Of young Guerin, the little French boy-peasant,
Who, being at a balloon-landing present,
The flying bag, with its hooked anchor, fished for,
Gave him as high a time as boy e'er wished for;
Clung to his waistbands, until fame it earned him,
Then gently to his parents' arms returned him
(Well known he is to balloon history-browsers,
This lad of tender years and sturdy trousers);
Of Thurston, who, his balloon sudden starting
A second trip, when from its basket parting,

Feared loss of what was costly in the getting,
And risked his life, and sprang into the netting;
And, as the sailor by his life-raft lingers,
Clung, until Death unclasped his freezing fingers;
Of Donaldson, who thought to spurn the ocean,
But found Lake Michigan a fatal potion;
Of Hogan, who, a new-made air-ship trying,
Straightway into eternity went flying;
And many others, Memory does not mention,
Secured this club's pictorial attention.

This club, whose zeal no cloak of age could smother,
Were very interesting to each other;
For all with strange, adventurous deeds were swelling,
Which pained them till divested of by telling;
And he who'd make five dollars contribution
(Which went to aeronauts in destitution)
Could tell a tale of half an hour's duration,
And three miles high; this was the limitation.
And he before correction's bar was cited,
Who went to sleep before the man alighted.

One winter night the chilly blast was crooning
Fierce odes against the science of ballooning,
And all out-doors with frosty burrs was bristling,
And loud the witches of the air were whistling,
And snow-squalls tried the windows till they trembled,
The club within their sanctum were assembled,
And one old sky-dog, having bought attention,
Achieved the following narrative-ascension:

THE CHILD-THIEF.

'Twas one fourth day of July,
With a deep blue, far-off sky,
And some north-east vapor-castles, built symmetrical and high;
And two small clouds, just a mile
Right above us, seemed to smile,
As to say, "Come up, poor earthlings, here, and visit us a while."

And the air was still and clear;
You could see and you could hear
Every little thing that happened, if the same was far or near;
And a crowd was standing by,
With investigating eye,
To assist in my departure for the regions of the sky.

I had filled my new balloon
Middle of the afternoon
(For it's never best to get off unprofessionally soon);
And she started like a queen
From the little village green,
And went up, and up, and upward, straight as ever you have seen!

'Twas a picture, I declare,
Rising through the summer fair,
Making for those pretty cloudlets, like two islands in the air;
And the earth began to seem
Like a distant, misty dream,
Full of farms and lakes and cities, and the river-silver-gleam;

And at last a current-gale
Struck my stately silken sail,
And I voyaged off to eastward, over mountain, hill, and vale,
Till I couldn't but understand
That a down-trip must be planned;
Though I came by air, a-flying, I must travel back by land!

Then I got myself in shape,
And I pulled the air-escape,
And my anchor through a forest 'gan to hitch and pull and scrape,
Till it caught an oaken knot
In a little forest lot,
And I found that I had landed in a very lonely spot.

Just a cabin-hovel nigh,
Not a single person by;
'Twas the loneliest bit of forest a balloonist could espy;

"AND MY LOVE AND PITY CLASPED HER, AND I COULD NOT LEAVE HER THERE."

And my nose wasn't over-fond
Of a little, stagnant pond,
And wherever glance could wander, rose the forest just beyond;

But a handsome little girl,
With her blue eyes all awhirl,
And her trim head ornamented by full many a golden curl,
From the hut came running out,
With a little, bird-like shout,
And embraced and kissed me, 'fore I quite knew what she was about;

"Oh, I knew you'd come," she said,
"From the country overhead,
Where my mamma went to visit when they told me she was dead;
For I prayed by day and night,
And then hoped with all my might,
She would send some one to take me into happiness and light!

"Since my uncle went away
To the 'Independence Day,'
I have knelt here, and done nothing but just pray and pray and pray;
And I've been expecting you
All the afternoon, for true,
Though I didn't suppose you'd get here just before the prayer was
    through!"

Then she showed me marks to spare
Of hard blows and cruel fare,
And my love and pity clasped her, and I could not leave her there;
I stopped kissing her, to say,
"I'm not going to heaven to-day,
And I don't believe that you will; but I'll start you, anyway."

And I drew her to me nigh,
And pulled up my anchor, spry,
And threw out some bags of ballast, and we sprang up toward the sky;
And she showed no sign of fright,
But went off to sleep all right,
And was sailing up in Dreamland, when we landed, just at night.

And I took a truthful plan,
When the kidnapping began,
And announced myself no angel, but a coarse and faulty man;
But she said she understood,
And she knew that I was good;
That her mother sent me for her, as she always knew she would.

And her uncle never knew
Where his little birdling flew,
Though I don't suppose he hunted more'n a century or two;
Didn't suspect that from above
I swooped down upon his dove,
And took off the little orphan that he hadn't the sense to love.

This sweet bit of ballast, she
Since has lived along with me,
And has loved me like a daughter, far as I could feel and see;
And if ever I can rise
Past the clouds, to Paradise,
It will be because that darling steers my soul into the skies.

————

The Club absorbed this fragment of narration,
With mild and rather frosty approbation;
Though now and then an old balloonist listened
With ears that heard, and eager eyes that glistened;
For pure love, in its ever-blessèd mission,
Strikes some old sinners' hearts with strange precision.
But most of them, polite attention feigning,
Found this mild tale not over-entertaining;
They wanted things unsafer and more thrilling—
Some sudden death, or close escape from killing;
And a young man the story-fee then tendered,
And this sad tale of love and death was rendered:

A LEAP FOR LOVE.

A great balloon hung in the city park,
Swelling and swaying with unconscious strength,

Grandly coquetting with the gentle breeze,
Then tugging at its leashes, with desire
To leap upon the clouds. A pleasure-throng
Struggled, and laughed, and waited for two souls
That soon would enter on a marriage tour,
In this strange wedding-car.

                And now there walked
Down a long lane, flesh-walled with living forms,
A bride and groom. Her classic-moulded face
Bore eyes half tender and half daring; as
Perchance the lioness Maid of Arc possessed.
Her wedding-gown was costless; but it gleamed
With the ne'er-stolen jewel of good taste;
And the hushed crowd gazed on her with respect.

The groom was strong and manly. Though his face
Clasped not the gift of beauty, yet it bore
The grander badge of manliness and brain.

Silence crept downward from the sky; and soon,
A man of God joined this adventuring two,
Whose souls already clasped. Then to the throng,
He pictured how the brave, determined pair
Were taking this strange flight, to win the means,
From those whose hands controlled the enterprise,
To launch their wedded life in prosperous seas.
At this the crowd cheered cheerily, and threw gifts;
And with proud smiles, 'mid bows of courtesy,
The pair embarked on their quaint wedding-tour.

The strands were cut; the buoyant engine climbed
Ladders of air; a chorus of hurrahs
Followed it, far as human voice could fly;
The silver sax-horns sung the Wedding March,
Which journeyed gayly with the wedded pair;
Glad church-bells swelled the stream of melody.

But soon were pierced the white walls of a cloud;
The wedded ones rose in the sun's clear light,
And found themselves alone, clasped hand in hand.

An hour they flew through the love-lighted air,
In converse close; past struggles were recalled,
To make more pure their present happiness;
They sundered seemed from every earthly care,
And felt as they had naught to do, but float
Forever through wide spaces, hand in hand,
And heart in heart; it seemed as if a world
Between the worlds—'twixt heaven and earth—were made
Into a new exclusive heaven for them,
Where they could live and love for evermore.

But when the sun began to seek the sea,
They knew that earthly life must re-begin;
He pulled the strand of rope that touched the valve.
Swift outward rushed the fluid that had borne
Them toward the sky—rushed farther toward the sky;
And downward sank the weight-borne bridal car,
And downward sank the love-bewildered pair.
The earth began to show its form once more,
And the sweet idyl of the air must end.

Still outward rushed the fluid that had borne
Them toward the sky—rushed farther toward the sky;
Still downward dashed the earth-desired balloon;
Still downward sank the fear-bewildered pair.
They strove to stop the valve, but 'twas in vain!
Some carelessness had plotted well with Death;
Earth was a grave, fast rushing up to them!

He flung the bags of ballast from the car;
He threw the outer garments they had worn;
He threw all weight that could be cut apart;
But it was vain: still to the earth they rushed—
A falling star of love and happiness!

At last, with intuition, born of thought,
And past experience, he divined the truth:
That but for his own weight, the falling mass
Would flutter, with no shock, unto the earth.

He clasped the bride a moment to his breast,
And whispered: "I have promised to protect
And shield you from all harm—even unto death;
My death means life for you; and here it is."

He kissed her lips, her brow, her eyes, her hands,
Then, without time for a detaining word,
Torn from her wild, beseeching, fainting grasp,
Sprang into the airy gulf.
                         Slowly she fell—
A pulseless form; but landed without hurt,
And walked for him in weeds for evermore.

———

The Sky Club heard this very sad recital,
With a display of pity almost vital;
And scarcely three through Dreamland had been soaring,
When it was done, and only one was snoring.
The Club gave these men (for its own protection)
The regular pecuniary correction;
Then for another story calmly waited.
At the established price already stated.

Not long; these proofs of Heaven's aerial mercies
(Especially the ones with well-filled purses),
Told several times, each one, the self-same story
(Not disconnected with the teller's glory),
And to reduce the cost were never trying,
Although, as one might say, at wholesale buying.
(Indeed, they always fined a fellow-rover,
Who told the same tale more than three times over.)

Soon rose a member with appearance youthful,
But whose unnumbered scars pronounced him truthful,
And for the second time began recalling
A reminiscence of stupendous falling,
When, self-announced, without a moment's warning,
An old man entered, salutation scorning,
Fastened the door as tight as bolt could lock it,
Retired the precious key into his pocket,

Then, on th' assembled people fiercely glaring,
With small regard for their indignant staring,
As there they sat, hot disapproval swallowing,
In feeble tones he shouted forth the following

FLIGHT OF THE AGED BALLOONIST.

You younger men, who loudly sing
  Old marvels night and day,
Now, listen while to you I bring
  Wise words from far away.

In yonder castle is my den:
  I dwell a hermit there,
Amid a lot of crazy men,
  O'er whom I watch and care.

These crazy men, some of them, too,
  Deem they do watch o'er me;
I let them think that thus they do,
  So quiet they may be.

I let them guard me through the day,
  I do as they have said;
These doctor-maniacs have their way,
  Till I be safe in bed.

And then—so soft and still I rise!
  I spurn this planet's ground;
My air-ship sails me to the skies,
  Where flocks of stars abound.

To tell you of the world of lune,
  Would take from youth to prime:
Last night I came back from the moon
  My fifty-second time.

And there I found a curious race,
  Who, when a man doth fall,

Toil hard to bring him back to place,
  Nor trample him at all.

Of Mars I have some tales to spare,
  Scant credence though you give:
The men who toil the hardest, there,
  Most sumptuously do live.

Word of what I in Saturn saw,
  Belief too seldom gains:
The people there who go to law,
  Get justice for their pains.

In Jupiter the man race are,
  Howe'er by wealth adorned,
Whenc'er they fall from Virtue's car,
  The same as woman scorned.

In Neptune I a story gat
  Few earthlings would indorse:
Men treat their bodies well as that
  Of any blooded horse.

In Venus is a sing'lar race,
  Who so acuteness lack,
They say the same things to one's face,
  They would behind his back.

In Mercury a lady lives,
  So to unselfness given,
She asks no pay for what she gives,
  Not even a crown in heaven.

In Uranus, last night, I heard
  Of men the same as I,
Who ne'er with look or deed or word
  Told any one a lie.

Within the nearest fixèd star—

At this the Sky Club made concerted motions,
Grappled the poor old peddler of high notions,
Fished out the key from his coarse, ragged pocket,
And fired him from the club-room like a rocket.

But lo! a new young man, with aspect tragic,
Came through the same door, like a trick of magic;
Two large revolvers in his hands were glistening,
Wherefore the Club began respectful listening.

A young balloonist of more sense than reason,
Who "went up" every day throughout the season;
And, far from earth, by baskets unobstructed,
A miniature circus of his own constructed;
And though in air well balanced, agile, ready,
On terra firma he was most unsteady;
Which fact was not entirely disconnected
With bibulous methods, which his face reflected.
He'd never wished to join the Sky Club's numbers,
And take part in their stories and their slumbers;
But loved, in slight fits of inebriation,
To burst in, bringing thrills of consternation.
He told of sundry new achievements clever,
Of the high calling they had left forever;
The many feats he had performed, though youthful,
All voiced in words unqualifiedly truthful;
He told of things these veterans, ere exempted
From all attempts, had never once attempted;
Of mounting up and sailing through the breezes,
Hung, not to baskets, but to frail trapezes;
Of summersaults, handsprings, etc., turning,
While earth and all such trivial matters spurning;
Of parachutes, to which, with vigor clinging,
He came down like a skylark from its singing;
And more things, calculated to make jealous
Some helplessly conservative old fellows.

At last a scarred balloonist faced the stranger,
In spite of imminent projectile danger,

And, with a look profoundly analytic,
Assumed the sombre functions of a critic,
And said: "This upstart's one of the possessors
Of ways unvouched for by his predecessors!
The idea of an artist young's pursuing
Things different from the things *we* have been doing!
His feats are new, and therefore inartistic,
And worthy no attention eulogistic.
And 'mid our walls, which helplessly enclose him,
I do hereby for membership propose him;
And to suspend the rules, so's to begin it—
Our voting for him—in about a minute;
And with blackballs, t' increase the information
Of this young jackanapes of innovation."

The o'er ambitious youth, with breath suspended,
This solemn voting with wide eyes attended;
Saw himself from a company rejected,
To which he'd never wished to be elected;
It was a thing that staggered his reflection—
This cold, unasked-for process of rejection;
The weight of precedence upon him bearing,
Depressed his spirits and destroyed his daring;
He soon sustained a low, crushed, humbled feeling,
And crept out, as if he had been caught stealing;
His body and his spirit both benighted,
And feeling that his whole career was blighted.

The Club then stretched, and yawned, and stretched—each vieing
With all the others, in relief-charged sighing;
Made fast the door, by chairs and tables aided,
As tightly as it could be barricaded;
And went on, harvesting the regular glories
Of the old-fashioned balloon-basket stories.

THE FESTIVAL OF THE FREAKS.

The Festival of the Freaks."

SCENE, *the main hall of a large "Dime Museum." Some space has been cleared for tables, and at the close of a particularly good day's business, the freaks are enjoying themselves at a supper given by the now-and-then liberal manager. Noises of street-cars and pedestrians heard faintly without. Queer things stare at them from the cases on the walls—curiosities staring at curiosities.*

PROPRIETOR.

Everything snugged up for night?

LECTURER.

All the sights are out of sight:
Mammoth curiosities,
Miniature monstrosities,
Things that sly old Nature made,
When in the constructing trade
She grew tired, as one might say,
Forming similar things each day,
And—with Fancy's sudden aid—
Fixed one up a different way;
All the whim-shaped quadrupeds,
All the calves with surplus heads,
All the plural-bodied lambs,
All the man-invented shams;
Things she double made, or half,
When she wished a little laugh;

All the things that thrill so much,
From great peoples' look and touch:
Bricks from near where they were born,
Clothes they've maybe some time worn;

6

Chairs their regal forms did hold;
Canes they lugged around when old;
Cradles of their helplessness;
Beds they've slept in more or less;

All the things that meet our views,
Of the toys that robbers use:
Slung-shot, nipper, jimmy, drill,
Blades whose edges yearned to kill;
False keys, billies, metal-fists,
Bracelets, forged for graceless wrists;
Saws, that tore some robber's way
From night-prisons into day;
Pistols, which in unfair strife
Robbed some half-waked man of life;
Locked up safely—all these nice
Curiosities of vice.

PROPRIETOR.

Snakes been housed and groomed and fed?

LECTURER.

All our pets are safe abed.
Coiled, the pictured rattlesnake,
Crawling weapon demons make,
To augment the world's distress:
Foe of timid helplessness—
Open poisoner of his foes—
Magazine of deadly blows.
Now he rests, with savage grace,
In a comrade's cold embrace.
Still, the boa's loathsome length,
Who, a chain of yielding strength,
Binds his prey to deathly doom,
Then becomes his living tomb.
Closed, the viper's brilliant eyes—
Maybe dreaming, as he lies,
Of old savage poisonous times,
In the sultry Eastern climes.

Safe are all these foes, designed
As the good friends of mankind,
Till, with purpose bad and deep,
Satan found their sire asleep.

PROPRIETOR.

Larger grows the list that you're
Yet unable to procure?

LECTURER.

Yes; a man who never yet
Uncontrolled temptation met;
And a woman who has never
Made uncelibate endeavor;
And a hero who has not
Borne some envy-furnished blot;
And a rich man who has never
Found a beggar over-clever;
And a youth who never sought
More attention than he ought;
And a saint who ne'er has been
Thinking how nice 'twere to sin;
And a mortal who admission
Never gained to superstition.

PROPRIETOR.

Then shall be our banquet spread;
Then the living freaks be fed;
Business ne'er has been so good
Since this wonder-temple stood;
Lucre-floods a week or more
Have been surging through our door—
Just as should be, when, with care,
All the realms of earth and air
Have been searched for what they owe
To a first-class moral show.
Set the tables, pour the wine!
All expense to-night is mine.

Flood the rooms with song and light;
Care a curio be to-night!
For one eve we'll happy be;
All expense shall fall on me!

LECTURER (*aside*).

Well, the boss struck a streak
Like he hasn't for many a week:
He's to-night his greatest freak!
Ne'ertheless my work, life through
Still, must be to help him do
What he thinks he wishes to.

———

SCENE II., *a well-spread table, covered with culinary débris, and surrounded with queer-looking people, of various colors, sizes, and weights.* PROPRIE-TOR *at head of the table.*

PROPRIETOR.

First we'll have a little song
From a veteran freak, who long
Up and down the country went,
With a museum side-show tent.
From the waving woods of Maine
To the sultry Texas plain;
From Atlantic billows cold,
To the western Gate of Gold;
While the circus raved and roared
To augment its treasure-hoard,
Making, with its giddy swirl,
The spectators' heads to whirl,
And with giddy thoughts affected,
With all wisdom disconnected,
He, apologist of lore,
In his tent's half-open door,
Stood, and, with an eloquence
Ciceronic and intense,
Begged the crowd to come inside,
Where, in pages opened wide,

"OH, I AM A SHOWMAN OLD,
UNCOMMONLY LARGE AND BOLD !"

Nature's wondrous curio-books
Would reward their eager looks,
And would give—by tact designed—
True instruction to the mind.

SONG OF THE SIDE-SHOWMAN.

Oh, I am a showman old,
  And I am a showman bold;
I stand outdoor an hour or more,
And point with pride to the things inside,
As I beseech, in eloquent speech,
That the crowd will see what things there be
Of those that stay in the far away,
And not forget Instruction's debt:
They laugh at me, and they chaff at me,
And I pay them back with the sudden crack
Of the lash of a word; and if they're stirred
  To give me a fistic stroke
  In pay for my little joke,

"Hey, Reub!" Hey, Reub! Hey, Reub!" says I;
They come from far an' they come from nigh.
"Hey, Reub! Hey, Reub! Hey, Reub!" reply,
An' each for each is ready to die.

Oh, I am a showman old,
  Uncommonly large and bold!
I stand outside with a gesture wide,
And speak up loud to the credulous crowd,
And tell what we desire 'em to see,
And maybe cut orf an inch o' the dwarf
And add some lies to the giant's size,
And tell in what part of Australia's heart
Was the wild boy born we caught one morn
With his woolly head in a Kansas bed!
The whole o' the truth I've told from youth,
Whatever betides, and more besides!

An' ever if unbelief
Is apt to bring me grief,

"Hey, Reub! Hey, Reub! Hey, Reub!" says I;
They come from far an' they come from nigh.
"Hey, Reub! Hey, Reub! Hey, Reub!" reply,
An' each is ready for each to die.

Oh, I am a showman old;
Perhaps you never was told
Concerning the row I sing of now,
A-circusin' late in Texas State:
Right in the crowd a fellow allowed
That cousin to me was the Chimpanzee.
I took a shy at his nearmost eye,
An' down he went like an egg in Lent!
His friends laid out to knock us about,
But 'twasn't a go—this whippin' a show;
We cleared 'em up, like flies in a cup—
I'd almost bet some lie there yet!
    There wasn't a minute to spare
    'Fore all our crowd was there!

"Hey, Reub! Hey, Reub! Hey, Reub!" says I;
They come from far an' they come from nigh.
"Hey, Reub! Hey, Reub! Hey, Reub!" they cry,
An' each was ready for each to die.

PROPRIETOR.

Here's a toast which I would give:
Long may all the short folks live!
Just a little room they take,
But a noise in th' world they make.
Who should take this toast to-night,
But our freaklet, General Slight?

INDIAN CHIEF (*aside*).

Why did pale-faced squaw let loose
Round here her old-man pappoose?

THE DWARF'S RESPONSE.

Reason that I'm here to-night
   No one here can help but know;
Plain to all discerning sight:
   Didn't grow.
Some who overgrew are here,
Some whose growth developed queer;
Some that grew themselves in ways
That from business stand-point pays;
All my charms are negative;
   How I've grieved the fact was so!
Though I just made out to live—
   Didn't grow.

Ate as much as any child,
   Climbed and tumbled high and low;
Still my friends in pity smiled—
   Didn't grow.
"He will take a start next year,"
Mother said, with half a tear;
Father growled, "Beyond a doubt,
Have to knead and stretch him out."
(Being a baker, he compared
   Body, if not head, to dough.)
Still the people downward stared—
   Didn't grow!

Went to school and joined my class—
   Toed a crack and joined a row;
Teacher croaked (the grim old ass):
   "Couldn't you grow?"
Tried to join in sports and games—
Never got beyond their names.
Though ten winters I could see,
Four-year-olds would bully me;
Stretched and ate, and o'er and o'er
   Swelled, frog-like, but 'twouldn't go;
More I undertook, the more
   Didn't grow.

Fell in love—as who has not,
    With love flitting to and fro?
But the same's a dreary lot,
    Till you grow.
Daily had to stand and see
Angel skyward creep from me;
Smiling on me from on high,
Pity in her distant eye;
Begged of her to wait a while
    Ere she took another beau;
Answered, with a pitying smile,
    "Darling, grow!"

So the world kept leaving me;
    Till folks said, "Why don't you grow
Up from small to greatest; see?
    Join a show."
Now I find that people pay
To see what they spurned away;
Now I think my purse would buy
Some who towered above me high;
She who "sacked" me as a lad,
    Now's my dearest, tallest foe;
Married me, and says she's glad
    Didn't grow.   *[Subdued applause.*

PROPRIETOR.

Here looms a giant, eight feet long,
Appropriately mild and strong.
Scorch with thy burning tongue the toast:
"Honor to him who grows the most!"

The GIANT *withdraws his feet from a position somewhere on the other side of the table, unpacks his
legs, stretches gradually toward the ceiling, steps
back two or three feet, frowns fiercely upon the
company, and proceeds, in a thin, piping voice:*

THE GIANT'S STORY.

The giant business isn't the thing at all
It used to be when I was somewhat small;
It's overdone, like every honest labor,
For any one an inch above his neighbor,
Tries hard to stretch to revenue-drawing length,
And coin up all his surplus into strength.
"Don't try it" is three words of good advice;
A giant earns his living over twice!

We have to stand and let the gaping crowd
Stare like a clock, and think of us out loud,
And ask us questions 'bout ourselves, till I
For one, am almost half-inclined to lie!
They grin us down with manners unrestrained,
Like as they would an elephant that's chained;
And every similar way they try to guide us,
Except to feed us peanuts and to ride us.

They ask us if the bulk in us they see,
Descended to us with our pedigree;
If when we're sick we suffer greater-wise
Than people of the regulation size;
How much per day or week our landlords charge;
If all our family are likewise large;
Being five times heavier than most human earth,
If we weighed forty-five pounds at our birth;
And other things, which, like domestic strife,
Look better in the depths of private life.
They make of every day a burden fresh,
A hundred times as weighty as our flesh.

They watch us when we walk to get the air,
The shouting kids pursue us everywhere;
They ask us if we still are growing tall;
How it affects things round us when we fall;
They play us tricks of different size and shape,
Then, dodging deftly 'twixt our legs, escape;

They ask is our maternal friend aware
That we have stepped into the open air;
And so we inconvenient hours must keep,
And walk at night, like people in their sleep.

But one of us, I always recollect,
Who made all people treat her with respect;
Her waist was fully fifteen feet around,
Her exhibition-weight six hundred pound.
And her home-heft, unpadded and sincere,
Would crowd five hundred, pretty middling near.

Though any chair she used, couldn't have a more
Unpaying contract than to guard the floor,
You never saw a form with willing grace,
You never saw a classic-moulded face,
You never saw a dame of high degree,
With any more true dignity than she;
There's only one man who, I ever heard,
Had cheek to give her an uncivil word;
And he ('tis hard that matters should go on so)
Was just the person that should not have done so.

I loved her—ain't ashamed to say it now;
She didn't me—God bless her, anyhow!
She had more solid sunshine in her eye,
Than I've discovered so far in the sky;
She held more information in her looks,
Than ever I have found in all the books;
She had more sympathy in voice and touch,
Than many folks who weighed a fifth as much!

I loved her—ain't ashamed to say it now;
She didn't me—God bless her, anyhow!
Perhaps she thought that happiness wouldn't seek
A family that contained too much physique;
Perhaps she let sweet pity get the start,
And found her judgment cornered by her heart;
I won't decide; I only know she strewed
Her young affections on a skeleton dude.

(I came near, in the midst of my dejection,
To breaking every bone in his collection!)

Heaven help her, then! he just let fly his growth,
And made her earn a living for them both!
He took to drinking, with enthusiasm fresh,
And didn't take any pains to curb his flesh;
And bigger every day he steady grew,
Until he hadn't a single rib in view
(Except his wife; and she'd grown thin and gray
If business matters hadn't stood in the way).

Now each new pound of meat the scamp displayed,
Was so much money chipped off from his trade;
Each inch diminished his professional art,
And piled lead in the poor fat lady's heart.
And she'd have pined away, she was so blue,
If only she could have afforded to.

Of course, the meaner that the scamp became,
The more she loved him (they are all the same,
Little or big), and he put up some new
Mean specialty for every breath he drew;
And soon became, as any one could see,
A large museum of what he shouldn't be.

Heaven help her, then! it's hard enough, I know,
For light-built folks to stand up under woe;
But 'tisn't every one that has to bear
Five hundred pounds of sorrow, in a chair.
It weighed upon my sweet and scornful friend,
Until the floor-planks almost seemed to bend;
But if true pity could have brought her round,
She wouldn't have tipped the scales at twenty pound.
Still, she in her own manner pined away,
And grew a little heavier every day.

This dude dove into every sort of sin,
And lined his skeleton outside and in;

Supported by his wife's industrious toil—
Oh, the scamp's coolness fairly made me boil!
It's very hard for any man that's human,
To see another man abuse a woman;
But awful hard his righteous rage to smother,
It's, when he hates the one and loves the other!

Till finally, one day, I spied a mark
Upon her neck—all swollen 'twas and dark;
And then I saw her sweet and mournful eyes
Were swelled with tears to half their usual size
(And her face being too large for actual need,
It made the eyes look very small, indeed);
And then I knew, what galls me in repeating:
He'd given his angel wife a first-class beating;
He'd struck and kicked her—fiends in fury lodge him!—
And she, being somewhat bulky, couldn't dodge him!

Murder was out; and nothing that could screen it—
I saw it all as plain as if I'd seen it!
And next time he nipped past my standing-station,
Strutting as if he owned the whole creation,
And the museum, and all the freaks there were—
Especially the body and soul of HER—
The hot steam of my hate grew so much stronger,
I couldn't endure the pressure any longer;
I collared him, spite of his puny groans,
And nearly shook the new flesh off his bones.

It made an interesting war-excitement,
Although the dude fool did not know what fight meant;
He limbered in—the little coward elf—
As if I was old giant Despair himself;
His heels flew up and nearly ripped in half
The sewed seams of the double-headed calf;
He hit the rope that strangled out the life
Of John J. Strong—the dude who killed his wife;
He broke a show-case, and brought down to grief
The handcuffs of a celebrated thief;

"I KICKED THE WHOLE ESTABLISHMENT WITH HIM."

He struck, and to the floor in ruins carried
A hung-up skeleton that wasn't married;
He made the monkeys' cage a casual call,
And furnished new excitement for them all;
He made a tune-box 'cross the room to roam,
That happened to be playing "Home, sweet Home;"
He sudden ran against, before he saw,
A Tipperary Injun and his squaw
(Whose savage souls straightway within them burned,
And so the greeting promptly was returned);
In short, being then in fair athletic trim,
I kicked the whole establishment with him.

The strangest part of all I now must say,
And, stranger still, it's generally that way:
This fellow's wife, that he'd used like a drum,
And marched her full half-way to kingdom come,
Defended him! And fell on me unbid
(And that meant something, weighing what she did),
And clapper-clawed me, till, she being done,
I had some thirteen bruises to her one.
(The dude stood by and saw this last occur—
Sponged even his vengeance on me out of her.)

In spite of all my rage and want of care,
He didn't seem a bit the worse for wear;
And made the judge believe 'twas all my fault,
And chuckled when they fined me for assault;
And his nibs said, "There's pity in this court
For one with such a large wife to support."

She died, a few years later than this row;
Died loving him—Heaven bless her, anyhow!

LECTURER.
Now let Whale-oil Jim be heard
In a little lyric word.

WHALE-OIL JIM *sings:*

THE SPECTRE WHALE.

I'll spin you a tale of a spectre whale
    That lives in the northern seas:
By night and day he swims, they say,
    Wherever he haps to please.
He haunts a ship all through her trip,
    Till stabbed by a luckless crew,
And then away, in the mist and spray,
    He tows them out of view.

    Then it's good-bye, shipmates,
        A thousand leagues you'll sail;
    Sing—hey—shipmates,
        You've caught the spectre whale!

I'll weep you a song of Captain Strong,
    A seaman tall and bold;
He swore he would slay that fish some day,
    And boil him in the hold.
But just as soon as the first harpoon
    Within his flesh was set,
They started away for Nowhere Bay,
    And maybe are sailing yet.

    Then good-bye, shipmates,
        Your friends they wonder and wail;
    Swim—fly—shipmates,
        You're caught by the spectre whale!

I'll laugh you a song of Peter Long,
    A first mate short was he;
He swore if he'd fail to catch the whale,
    That Satan's he would be!
But first we knew, it opened to view
    Its mouth so wide and strong,
And caught him fast, and that was the last
    We saw of Peter Long.

Then good-bye, shipmates,
    You'll take a Jonah-sail;
Soft lie, shipmate,
    Your berth, the spectre whale!

I'll heave you a word of Nicholas Bird,
    A foc'sle liar was he—
Showed part of the tail of the ghost's own whale
    That he killed in '53.
He finally said, "When I am dead
    My ghost will give him a try,
And that I say is the only way
    The spectre fish can die."

Then fare you well, shipmate,
    For if you did not lie,
Too much truth to tell, shipmate,
    Is just as bad, or nigh.

We grappled the man by a sudden plan
    (A struggling fish was he)!
And, begging his ghost to perform its boast,
    Flung Nicholas in the sea.
And oft at night he is seen by the light
    Of the miracle-loving moon,
To chase the whale, through calm or gale,
    With the ghost of his old harpoon.

Then good-bye, shipmate,
    And if your ghost should fail
Itself to die, shipmate,
    Perhaps you'll catch the whale.

LECTURER.
Here's the young discouraged wight,
Who, one afternoon or night,
Hoping that his life, sore blighted,
Could, by wronging it, be righted;
Thinking, if for sorrow's sake,
He his sad career might break,

Through some fate it might be mended,
From the mammoth bridge descended,
And, by guardian angels guided,
Head-first in the water glided;
Through the awful danger skimming
Like a truant boy "in swimming."
Let him now, in private glory,
Tell once more his public story.

> [*The* BRIDGE-JUMPER *arises amid wild applause, not
> being a freak by birth, hence not having displayed
> sufficient attraction to arouse envy. He is an in-
> offensive little fellow, with an exceedingly sad face.*

THE BRIDGE-JUMPER'S STORY.

Oh, who can tell what spirit brought
   To earth that firebrand Suicide,
Or whose insanity first taught
   The art to those whose courage died,
And lived again in coarser thought?
   The selfish crime doth still abide,
   And murders mortals far and wide.

Oh, who describes the dark despair
   That falls in floods upon the heart,
And drowns in blood the healthy care
   That breeds employment's cheerful art;
Then clogs the tempest-shrieking air
   With terror's swiftly-flying dart,
   To force the frenzied brain apart?

Oh, who can count the many woes
   To which the lonely crime is traced?
The lovers false, the genuine foes,
   The staining lash of foul disgrace.
Gaunt poverty's heart-weakening blows,
   Red dissipation's prizeless race,
   And lunacy's uncouth embrace?

Oh, who can tell the thoughts of him
   Who knows that in a second's time
His earthly eyes must stagger dim,
   His soul desert the earthly clime—
He hopes life's lamp once more to trim,
   He fears, to plunge through depthless slime
   And drag the fetters of his crime!

He knows not whether pitying friends
   May meet him at the shattered door,
And with their kindness make amends,
   For fate, of what has gone before,
And aid the mercy Heaven extends
   To stanch his pain-charged spirit-gore,
   And soothe him sweetly evermore;

Or whether he be doomed to bear
   The finger-tip of cruel scorn,
And in the silent spirit-air
   May hear the words, "A coward born!"
As, followed by a new despair,
   O'er roads beset with poisoned thorn,
   He runs a race of rage forlorn;

Or whether, o'er his troubled soul,
   Oblivion as a mercy creeps,
And guards him out of care's control
   Within its broad, mysterious deeps;
And thus while years above him roll,
   He free from pain and pleasure sleeps,
   And time's deep ocean o'er him sweeps;

Or whether from this plunge of fate
   He sinks in valleys red with fire,
Inhabited by fiends of hate—
   New cruelties their sole desire—
Who hope their sufferings to abate
   By helping hell's demoniac ire
   To make his sufferings yet more dire!

And who can tell how long he thought
   And brooded o'er his deadly scheme,
And webs of fact and fancy wrought
   To make the project easy seem;
And his weak muscles courage taught,
   By his despairing spirit's scream,
   In daylight's thought and midnight's dream;

And who can tell, when the frail cord
   That holds his life once loose is thrown,
And helplessly he rushes toward
   The unescapable unknown,
How suddenly is now abhorred
   The death he sought in moments flown; . .
   If life once more could be his own!

If yet again he could but try
   This world's rough tangle to make straight!
A hundred methods meet his eye
   To open rescue's gilded gate;
A thousand griefs that, when so nigh,
   So heavy—now have little weight;
   Could he but live, now 'tis too late!

And all the pages of his life
   Turn, rustling, in his opening brain:
The love, the hate, the peace, the strife,
   The hope, the grief, the loss, the gain;
Once more disease's hiltless knife—
   Once more the joy of banished pain;
   The good, the bad, the true, the vain;

He lives a lifetime of despair
   Between his dying and his death;
As, crucified, he lingers there,
   A loud voice drowns his burdened breath:
"Mercy in earth or Heaven or air
   Is not for him who blasphemeth
   Against God's image!" Thus it saith.

So when I leaped from yonder span,
    In death my burning soul to lave,
Hot demons through the spirit ran,
    And held me as their suffering slave.
A long eternity began;
    And every instant was a grave,
    That pain, instead of slumber, gave.

An instant may be made a year;
    A second's thousandth million part
May be an age of pain and fear,
    Whose every moment probes the heart;
And many heavens or hells can here
    Be lived, ere for the land we start,
    Whose borders know no earthly chart.

God brought me back; 'twas thus that I
    Once more life's honeyed air could sip;
He somehow heard my silent cry,
    Recalled me in the deathward trip,
And brought me back once more to try,
    With streaming face and pallid lip,
    Eternity's apprenticeship.

This trembling world doth not contain—
    However deep, however wide—
Enough of sorrow, fright, or pain,
    Or woe unknown, or grief untried,
Or frost of heart, or fire of brain,
    Or anything—to drive or guide
    My steps again to suicide!

I stand before the gazing throng,
    Not for the paltry gain of purse:
To pray them not from shame or wrong
    To fly to evils that are worse.
And hoping, as my race among,
    This hideous story I rehearse,
    That God may stay the selfish curse.

PROPRIETOR.

Doleful tale is that, indeed!
Let us all take wholesome heed,
Striving not to lose our lives,
Till the proper time arrives.
And, meanwhile, for order's sake,
Let each listener now awake,
While a story sweetly flits
From the Bearded Lady's lips.

> [*The* BEARDED LADY *rises shyly, throws back some
> masses of raven hair, parted in the middle, grooms
> a luxuriant beard and mustache with eight taper-
> ing fingers, blushes slightly, and proceeds.*

THE BEARDED LADY'S STORY.

When woman out of man was made,
Where she in ambush had been laid;
When, with Heaven's wisdom for a guide,
She crept forth from her husband's side,
Part of him, yet not all his own,
A dream of flesh and blood and bone
(And ever since has been, 'twould seem,
His cherished and evasive dream,
And—as I hardly need to mention—
The constant bone of his contention);
When, thrilled with intuition's lore,
She looked the situation o'er,
And saw how weak she was, compared
To him who with the world she shared;
Saw how each gesture of his hand
Her goings and comings might command;
Saw how, Heaven's purpose to fulfil,
Her motions leaned upon his will;
She made her mind up, that same hour,
That she must wield a different power;
That she must gain her motives' length,
By indirect and subtle strength.
And, glancing in a pool, saw she
Was so much handsomer than he,

She beauty's cord might round him tie,
And thus the lack of strength supply;
And so she made, with motive good,
Herself as handsome as she could.

Indeed (although I've sometimes thought
My thought oft thinks more than it ought)
I've thought sometimes that half the reason
She coaxed young Adam into treason
Against Divinity's command,
To take the apple from her hand,
Was her prophetic vision, staring
At herself, gorgeous dresses wearing,
When fig-trees, other trees, and all
The birds and beasts would come at call,
And by the aid of artists clever,
Would make her handsomer than ever.
Flounces and ribbons are a prize
In any regular lady's eyes;
And good appearance, in her heart,
Of good religion is a part.

This being truth, you'll easy know
Why 'tis that woman suffers so,
When nature takes a sudden whim,
And tricks her out in masculine trim,
Making her (if a little pun
Just slipped in here for my own fun
Won't lower me in your regard)
Mustached and bearded like her pard.
Some, lotions use, to stop its growth,
And peel off skin and whiskers both;
With tweezers uncombined with ruth,
Some draw them like an aching tooth;
To keep their dreadful secret sure,
Some surreptitiously procure
Razor and soap—sly, honest plan—
And meet the trouble like a man;
But each must always watch and doubt,
For fear their hair will find them out.

One such as this I knew of well
(Although her name I'd scorn to tell,
For not alone does queer old Nature's
Quaint mind have whims about our features;
We bearded ladies gossip smother,
And always stand up for each other):
This lady was a teacher fair—
A principal; and with great care
Watched close a school, it would appear did,
Composed of several girls, unbearded;
And strove, she said, they might not stray
One hair's-breadth from the narrow way.

But several neighboring student-boys,
Debarred by her from social joys,
Which they fallaciously deemed due
(The girls concurring in that view),
Marked slyly as their mischief's own,
This razor-wielding chaperon;
And in a sneaking manner then
Resolved to beard her in her den;
And on one Halloween they stole
A large and lurid barber-pole,
And, more in anger than in wit,
Beneath her window fastened it,
In such unprecedented way
'Twould not be moved till noon next day—
A target for by-passers' questions,
And sly tonsorial suggestions.
In fact, the symbol, as it proved,
Could never somehow quite be moved;
It was a shame ridiculous,
To treat a bearded lady thus!

And still if she, I can but say,
Had just let Nature have its way,
And not clipped off the strands it spun,
But helped them, as she might have done,
She could have been a first-class freak,
And made more money in a week,

Than in a whole scholastic year;—
But, then, we women folks are queer.

Until she moved some distance, where
Unknown yet was her face and hair;
And she, this guiltless shame above,
Could prosecute her work of love.
Her pupils day by day she taught
With precept kind and subtle thought,
And ne'er appeared with any trace
Of manhood on her thoughtful face;
Her mild, sharp practice not detected,
And, as she prayed, still unsuspected;
Although in various times and shapes
She'd several close hair-breadth escapes.
She did her work well as she could,
And all but rivals called it good.

And she had hoped to live her life
Alone, Industry's faithful wife;
And the staid, solemn comfort felt,
Of those to whom no man has knelt;
And who, no doubt, will e'er escape
All interference of that shape;
Was gathering fast the curious ways
That antique maiden life displays;
And settling down, the strands to weave,
Of a long quiet winter eve.

When, presto! came a comely man,
Who, by well-laid heroic plan,
And Love's sly, sinless, treacherous art,
Found means to trap her virgin heart!
And with imperious methods bland,
Humbly petitioned for her hand.

What now? Love promptly took the field,
And wildly pleaded her to yield;
Tired loneliness its woes enlarged,
And humbly begged to be discharged;

Old age peeped at her—most in sight—
And holloed "Yes!" with all his might;
Ambition made a lively speech,
Wherein he did not fail to reach
A rival maid her lover knew,
And artfully had held in view;
And Comfort—sweet her voice did blend—
Said, "Let me be your friend, my friend!"
But tired Despair, with hopeless frown,
Pointed a fateful finger down,
Where 'twixt the lovers had been laid
A sharp and fiercely gleaming blade;
And that was, as you'll easy guess,
A razor—mirror of distress!

What should she do then? Wed her lover?
Then he The Secret might discover,
And every sympathy refuse,
And she his scared affections lose.
And if she firmly answered "Nay,"
Then she would lose him anyway.
And so for weeks she vacillated
Whether to be or be not mated.

At last a bright idea occurred:
She wrote The Secret, every word,
Enclosed it to him in a letter,
And felt disconsolate, but better.
Then, like a prisoner mystery-fated,
She for his answer watched and waited.

She waited well; a week went by,
Also her hope of quick reply.
She waited long; a month appeared,
But brought no reference to her beard.
And 'twas a campaign every day,
Through student ranks to fight her way—
To train youth's talent into art,
Pipe off the gushes of the heart,

And proffer pearls of greatest price
In golden caskets of advice;
The tune of others' heart-strings taking,
The while her own were slowly breaking;
And, treading life's rough pathway o'er,
Shave regularly as before.

At last, one eve, a package came,
That bore her chaste baptismal name,
In a loved hand she knew so well!
And—let me now its contents tell:
A brush of rare and dainty mould;
A shaving-cup of purest gold;
A razor, in whose haft of jet
Large diamonds and pearls were set;
A hand-glass, whose fine ivory frame
In ruby letters bore her name;
And other things, such as form part
Of amateur tonsorial art;
Whose terms I cannot call to mind,
Using no utensils of that kind.

But maybe you have not surmised
The treasures she most dearly prized:
Her first love-letter! which contained
This flood of passion unrestrained:
"Dearest of maids! I now unfold
A secret until here untold:
When those wild students basely reared
A monument unto your beard,
Thus laying on your shrinking soul
A large ten-dollar barber-pole,
I was the barber, and reveal it,
From whom the scamps bought leave to steal it.
But seeing you bore with such sweet grace
Those coarse allusions to your face,
How bravely you ignored the slur,
How patient, meek, and kind you were,
And yet how like a stricken deer
You fled in grief, if not in fear,

I loved you deeply, and pursued;
Found, met, loved better still, and wooed.
Your facial gifts I loved—not braved;
Besides, you see, my mother shaved.
And, life being made financial summer
By uncle's death (a cold-snap plumber),
My being's sole object, I confess,
Is your joy, peace, and happiness.
Knowing the fact your letter stated,
Still for your word I hoped and waited;
And see you now one whose sweet heart
Would nothing keep from me apart."

They married; and, in checkered cheer,
Lived happily for many a year.
She proved a solace in his life—
A faithful, kind, instructive wife;
And he from earth's rude contact saved her,
And every morning neatly shaved her.

PROPRIETOR.
Moral: let the truth prevail,
Though the heavens and earth may fail;
Though for love's endearments pleading,
Love lies wounded, sick, and bleeding.
Nothing holds, in age or youth,
Like the firm, old-fashioned truth;
Nothing long can stand in place,
If truth be not at the base.

LECTURER.
Truth! a curio that is worth
All the others on this earth.

THE DISABLED BALLOONIST (*who has made five hundred and sixty-seven successful ascensions, and one unsuccessful one*).
Truth! the only star whose ray
Shines the brighter when 'tis day!

DWARF.

> Truth! though sometimes small to see,
> Greatness hath her home in thee!

GIANT.

> Truth! whose strength in field or town,
> Tears all worthless structures down!

FIRST ALBINO.

> Truth! a maid whose eyes sincere,
> As the mountain brook are clear!

INDIAN CHIEF (*aside*).

> Truth! Humph! Ugh! A great big mound,
> Where no white man's scalp is found!

THE SWORD-EATER.

> Truth! whose blade of brightest hue
> Cleaves the false and spares the true!

THE JUGGLER.

> Truth! whose oft-secreted ball
> Comes up finally top of all!

THE ARMLESS MAN.

> Truth! in genuine fabric shows,
> Made with fingers or with toes!

THE FASTER.

> Truth! a table thickly spread,
> Where all hungry may be fed!

THE SNAKE-CHARMER.

> Truth! on whose magnetic arm
> Serpents wind and do no harm!

BEARDED LADY.

> Truth! when I to live, must lie,
> Guardian angels, let me die!

[*A footstep in the hall. The door opens with a bang;
a large, resolute, but frightened-looking woman
enters, and glares sharply up and down the room.
The* BEARDED LADY *creeps under the table.*

FRIGHTENED BUT RESOLUTE-LOOKING WOMAN.

Lost! Lost! Lost! My husband's lost!
On my lonely bed I've tossed,
Fighting desperation's power,
Waiting for him hour by hour,
Till suspense paled into fear.
Say, freaks, is not my freak here?
Do admit me to him, pray!
Prayers shall for my ticket pay!
Or if he has cut the show,
Tell me where he said he'd go,
So I there no time may waste,
And through other haunts may haste!

[*She catches a glimpse of the* BEARDED LADY *under
the table.*

There he is—cheek, lip, and chin;
Drunk once more, as sure as sin!

[*Hauls him from under the table by hair and beard.*

Stagger! for your road is broad!
Oh, you hair-faced, bare-faced fraud!
Here's your shawl and bonnet, see?
Now, sir, travel home with me!

[*She leads him away, somewhat sobered and very
much subdued.*

PROPRIETOR.

Beat that, any one who can!

INDIAN CHIEF.

Humph! the chin-scalp squaw's a man!

THE FESTIVAL OF THE TRAM CLUB.

The Festival of the Tram Club.

CONDUCTOR.

Comrades of this festival,
Is there one who can recall
Ancient snail-drawn stage-coach days,
Ere, by metal-bordered ways,
The life-crowded lightning-train,
Trampling loud from plain to plain,
Bearing its own steed of steam,
Was a truth, and not a dream?
Ere through storms or gleams of day,
Flying cities sped their way;
Ere, by night, the brilliant cars,
Like a stream of shooting-stars,
Yet inhabited by man,
Their swift pageantry began?

BAGGAGE-MAN.

A MODERN CASSANDRA.

Yes; I can recollect a time, when, if I had suggested
That things like cars would ever be, I'd almost been arrested.
Before they'd let a fellow make a prophecy much hazier,
They'd put him in asylum walls, and maybe make him crazier.
There's toleration for a man behind the times, some distance;
But any one that's far ahead—he won't enjoy existence.

Now there was Ruby Willoughby: as fine a girl as often
Kept twenty fellows cooing round, her heart toward them to soften.
She 'tended the debating-schools, much sage instruction gaining,
And heard all subjects there discussed, to earth and heaven pertaining;

But as for making speeches, then—girls never used to do it,
Being not supposed to say a thing, however well they knew it.
(They're more like men are, nowadays, *my* observation teaches;
The less they know about a thing, the longer are their speeches.)

One evening, when the theme picked out to steer the disagreeings,
Was whether iron or gold was most of use to human beings,
Each speaker was assigned his views on this important matter,
And not a single first-class speech had cut through the clatter,
A young chap raised his safety-valve—a handsome, wholesome fellow
As ever made a maiden's heart love-ripen till 'twas mellow;
A regular Patrick Henry speech he made as Iron's attorney,
And scraped the sky, and all the crowd went with him on the journey;
My very hair stood up to hear the chap's sublime oration.
(Insurance agency became his ultimate vocation.)

And Ruby sat and looked at him, her head by little raising,
And her blue eyes grew dark like night, and then burst out a-blazing
(She oft had traded looks with him, as if she meant to mean them,
And something more and less than space was thought to be between
     them);
And when he'd finished, she arose, wrapped in a frenzied flurry,
And, shouting "I will prophesy!" went at it in a hurry.

"I see," she said, "in yonder vale a horse of iron go speeding,
And bushels oft of blazing coals are measured for his feeding!
His head is iron, his body iron, his feet—the earth while scorning—
His breath is like the chimney-smoke upon a winter morning!
He's harnessed up in brass and steel, the buckles wide and gleaming;
His neigh is like the autumn gales when through the forest screaming!

"I see a dozen carriages behind him swiftly running,
All full of comfort and of light, and trimmed with dexterous cunning;
Like flying cottages they look, with palace-splendors gliding;
But travellers walk about in them, as if at home residing!
All things seem for their comfort made, quick met are all their wishes.
I see the flutter of their beds, the gleaming of their dishes.
They read, they write, they stitch, they laugh—all in the flying car-
     riage;
They even spin the tender threads that weave the strands of marriage!

"I talk with one whose sable hue proclaims a bondsman lowly,
Yet with a haughty-humble air he answers questions slowly.
I ask him if the horse is his; his ample lip grows shorter;
He answers, 'Not exactly, miss, but I'm the Pullman porter.'
What this may mean I do not know; but people who'd live gayly,
Submit to him with deference, and pay him tribute daily.

"He tells me that some travellers there, are sad of heart and feature,
Because they are not 'up on time,' or something of that nature;
Five hundred miles they've journeyed since the sun's last previous
    setting;
They'll come to Boston 'three hours late,' and that is why they're
    fretting.
They sit and sulk while drawn by hoofs that well might drown the
    thunder,
And murmur and repine, instead of being dazed with wonder!

"They still complain—heavens, what is that! the horse is reeling—
    stumbling!
Beneath his clattering steel-shod feet, the iron road is crumbling!
A crash—a blaze like burning clouds in thunder-beaten weather—
Horse, rider, travellers, carriages—all crush and crash together!
Pain! Blood! Death! Help!"—the prophetess with consciousness
    grew weaker,
And fell into the willing arms of the preceding speaker.

So it became a legend-joke—the fact of Ruby's vision—
Until at last a fact appeared with terrible precision:
A railroad through that valley runs, in just the same direction
She pointed at, the night she made her strange tour of inspection:
Also a railroad accident, with Horror's hand to mould it,
Occurred, one night, not half a mile from where the girl foretold it.

CONDUCTOR.

Sailors through the hills and dales,
Is one here can tell us tales
Of those times when doubting man
First to "railroad it" began?
When the giant Steam's employ,
Was, to move a toiling toy?

8

When a "train of cars" would seem
O'ergrown wagons pushed by steam?
When most mortals did not know
Whether railroading would "go,"
Or rest in the weary round
Of things "tried and wanting" found?

TRAIN-DESPATCHER *reads*:

JONATHAN JARVIS.

Now ponder long, ye comrades dear,
   The tale that I shall tell,
Of Jonathan Jarvis, Engineer,
   And things that him befell;
And learn from this, 'tis oft amiss
   To do your work too well.

'Twas in a stormy time o' the year,
   In the fall of forty-two,
That Jonathan Jarvis, Engineer,
   As he was wont to do,
Had just begun to take his run
   To the town of Kalamazoo.

His engine was of largest stripe
   That so far had been made;
The smoke-stack big as a chimney-pipe—
   The whole five hundred weighed;
And it could go twelve miles or so,
   Per hour, adown a grade.

The whistle it did sound as loud
   And startling-like, and shrill,
As boys, with jack-knives bright endowed,
   Of bass-wood carved with skill,
And never a bell to ring the knell
   Of those the cars might kill.

The driving-wheels were large as those
  Upon a wagon small;
And we may naturally suppose
  That there were four in all;
And four were there, that box to bear
  That they the tender call.

And Jonathan Jarvis, Engineer,
  Was full of worthy pride;
He was a popular man, and dear
  To all that country-side;
And every boy was wild with joy,
  That could with Jonathan ride.

It was a sight to see the train
  The country thundering through;
And maidens fair as maids could be,
  Ran all of the doors unto;
But Jonathan yet, with teeth firm set,
  Kept on for Kalamazoo.

Eftsoon a terrible storm uprose,
  Of thunder and lightning, too;
The air was full of flood and flame,
  The sky yet blacker grew;
But Jonathan still, with iron will,
  Kept on for Kalamazoo.

The storm sped on with all its might;
  It made immense display;
With whirring wings the raven Night
  Flew into the lap of Day;
But Jonathan still, with iron will,
  Kept on his wooden " way.

The wind it roared and cried and laughed,
  The rain in billows flew;
They tried to wreck the small land-craft;
  But Jonathan, fiercely true,

Still strove to make, for Duty's sake,
    The port of Kalamazoo.

A blue light over the smoke-stack hung,
    As oft upon a mast;
The rain-drops to the boiler clung,
    And strove to hold there, fast;
And gaudily dire great balls of fire
    Along the railway passed.

The cars of the train, they all unhitched
    (One coupling strength did lack),
And down a grade, as if bewitched,
    They all went skurrying back;
But Jonathan yet, with teeth firm set,
    Kept up the slippery track.

The engine tipped and creaked and groaned,
    As might a ship at sea,
And like a living animal moaned,
    And strove to struggle free,
And soon appeared with wheels upreared
    Against a fallen tree.

Then Jonathan Jarvis did a deed
    Like loftier men oft do:
His good umbrella spread with speed;
    And, first his fireman knew,
With one fierce shout, he started out
    Afoot, for Kalamazoo.

"Come back!" his fireman yelled; "Come back!"
    With many a loud halloo;
But still he hurried up the track,
    With purpose born anew,
And said, "I'll break my neck, or make
    The town of Kalamazoo!"

And some time on the following day,
    And blind, and deaf, and lame,

A bootless tramp, half-blown away,
  Into the station came,
Who yelled in glee, "Excelsior! See?
  I got here, just the same!"

Umbrella and hat, they both were gone,
  His vestments showed but few,
And every rag that he had on,
  The storm had whipped in two;
A scurvier wight, by day or night,
  Ne'er entered Kalamazoo.

You see he lost, some distance back,
  His engine, train, and crew;
Left most of himself along the track,
  His purpose to pursue;
Even lost his head; but gained, instead,
  The town of Kalamazoo.

And many a man on life's long road,
  Has toiled to "get" somewhere,
And left, while onward still he strode,
  All things both good and fair,
And reached the spot, and found that not
  One-tenth of himself was there.

CONDUCTOR.

    Flyers, with strong wings of steel,
    Is there one who can reveal
    That he saw, 'gainst earth or skies,
    Railroad apparitions rise?
    Met a straggler from the hosts
    Of the flesh-divested ghosts,
    That in sorrow walk the earth,
    Clinging where their woes had birth?
    In our nerve-exciting rounds
    Oft are curious sights and sounds;
    If one be here who can tell
    Such a story, do it well.

All are gazing at yon brown
Engine-driver, shrinking down,
Who believes that phantoms live.
Rise, ghost-advocate, and give
Us to hear the privilege,
Of the ghost of Breakneck Bridge!

THE ENGINE-DRIVER'S STORY.

Since you're all bearin' down on me, and won't let me up without it,
    I'll tell you a story, providin' you'll let me foller my plan;
Nor I sha'n't fly the track, although you appear to doubt it,
    But push ahead to my station as fast as ever I can.

Company, please excuse me fur all my gropin' an' skippin';
    Likewise from whistlin' at crossin's, or makin' stops to explain;
Never was on the explain; it sets a man's drivers to slippin',
    Wherefore he's sure to be losin' more time than he'll ever gain.

Johnny McNutt was my fireman: as fine young feller as ever
    Planted his hoof on a foot-board, or swore at sulphury coal;
Al'ays in his place, an' 'Merican meanin' of clever,
    Without any gage on his pockets, or steam-brake onto his soul.

Johnny, he had a wife: she somehow must ha' bewitched him,
    Fur she was old an' ugly—how old I do not know;
The boys was al'ays wonderin' as how she ever had switched him;
    But it was a dead-true certain, for she had the orders to show.

Twenty times he had switched her, an' left the old gal behind him;
    Twenty times she had followed, an' stuck to him like a burr;
Wherever he might run, she was always sure to 'find him;
    For, poor old soul, she loved him, although he couldn't her.

All the "legal" remedies that surfeited folks is tryin'
    Johnny took no stock in; he sent her half his pay!
An' though the lawyers offered a square divorce for the buyin',
    He made no run for freedom, except to keep out of her way.

"EVERY ONCE IN A SHORT TIME SHE'D COME UPON US QUICK."

Now when John fired with me, he was feelin' some'at better,
  An' somehow had an ide' he'd nothin' more to fear;
For he'd seen nothin' of her—not even the ghost of a letter,
  As he in confidence told me—for somethin' more than a year.

But just as we was a-startin' one night from a one-hoss station,
  She climbed up onto the foot-board, a-lookin' wrinkled an' wan,
An' went for John, an' hugged him an' kissed him like all creation!
  An' the more he tried to shake her, the more the old gal hung on!

Breakneck Bridge is a matter of fifty foot from the bottom;
  Nothin' when you've got there, except the rock an' sand;
An' just as we struck the centre, as if the old boy had got 'em,
  They both went off together, before I could raise a hand!

Off in the pitch-black darkness, they both of 'em went a-flyin';
  Off in the pitch-black darkness, they both pulled out for Death;
An' when we found 'em, the woman was down on the rocks a-dyin'
  An' John had catched on a timber, mashed up an' out o' breath.

An' Johnny laid off for repairs, an' full for a year I missed him;
  But very first time he was able to make his run once more,
Sir, the ghost of a wrinkled woman climbed up in the cab an' kissed him,
  An' when we got to the Breakneck Bridge, went off, as *she* did
    before.

I knowed when I opened my valves that you'd some on you disbe-
    lieve me,
  Though why you should, I'm certain is more than I can think;
For eyes ain't tongues, an' mine don't often go to deceive me,
  An' I never doused my head-light with any kind of drink;

Sir, so that singular woman run down on us all summer;
  Every once in a short time she'd come upon us quick;
Till John remarked to me, "There's no escapin' from her;
  I'll have to leave the engine; I'm gettin' tired an' sick."

An' afterwards he wrote me: "If I can believe my senses,
  I see my wrinkled woman wherever I may go;

I reckon she's got a pass; an' how to pay expenses,
　　And keep away from a deadhead, is rather more'n I know."

From which I have learned this lesson: Be sure and never try for 't
　　To run from a desperate woman that thinks she's treated wrong;
She'll follow you up an' catch you, although she has to die for 't;
　　For love an' hate together can pull exceedin' strong.

Sir, that's the whole of my story; I've tried hard not to wander,
　　An' done my best t' work steady and keep her up on time;
An' I shall be somewhat suited, unless that feller yonder
　　Steams up his poetical b'iler an' runs me into rhyme.

CONDUCTOR.

Sailors of the iron seas,
Accidents and dire disease
Oft afflict our toiling band; '
Many a sturdy heart and hand
Low in cemeteries lie,
Past which they were wont to fly,
Knowing, in gay carelessness,
Naught of danger or distress;
Counting no long weeks of pain
In life-struggles sadly vain;
With no fear of lying dead
'Neath the engine's heavy tread;
Thinking naught how soon the places
That had glimpsed their smiling faces,
As they journeyed to and fro,
Others in their place must know;
Is there one within the room,
Who will voice that thought of gloom?

SUPERINTENDENT.

UNDER THE WHEELS.

I have had many hard things to do in my day,
　　For the life of "the boss" isn't constructed of play;
We've a hundred new things every hour to annoy,
　　And we work more than any one in our employ.

But the hardest day's work I remember to-night,
Was to visit a cottage, clean, cosey, and bright,
Where flowers, birds, and music were strewn without lack,
And to carry some news that should drape it with black.
A sweet-faced old lady my door-signal met,
And gave me these words—I shall never forget,
If I live till Time's wheel has crushed all things at last,
And railroads and progress are things of the past:

" You've called to see Jack, I suppose, sir; sit down;
I'm sorry to say 't, but the boy's out of town.
He'll be back in an hour, if his train is not late,
And perhaps you'd be willing to sit here and wait,
While I give you a cup of his favorite tea,
Almost ready to pour.—Oh!—you called to see me?
You—called—to—see—me? Strange—I didn't understand;
But, you know, we old ladies aren't much in demand;

" You—called—to—see—me. And your business is—Say!
Let me know now at once! Do not keep it away
For an instant! Oh!—pardon! You wanted to buy
Our poor little house here? Now thank God on high
That it wasn't something else that you came for!—shake hands;
    I'm so glad!—and forgive an old woman's ado,
While I tell you the facts, till your heart understands
    The reason I spoke up so brusquely to you:

" My life lives with Jack!—a plain boy, I confess—
He's a young engineer on the lightning express;
But he loves me so true! and though often we part,
He never 'pulls out' of one station—my heart.
Poor Jack! how he works! He sinks into this chair,
    When he comes home, so tired with the jar and the whirl;
But he fondles my hands and caresses my hair,
    And he calls me his 'love,' and his 'darling best girl.'
Poor Jack! but to-morrow is Christmas, you know,
    And here is his present: a gown of fine wool,
Embroidered with silk; my old fingers ran slow,
    But my heart filled the stitches with love over-full!

"So, when Jack is gone out on his dangerous trip,
 On that hot, hissing furnace that flies through the air,
Over bridges that tremble, past sidings that slip,
 Through tunnels that grasp for his life with their snare,
I think of him always—I'm never at rest.
 And last night—O God's mercy!—the dreams made me see
My boy lying crushed, with a wheel on his breast,
 And a face full of agony beck'ning to me!
Now, to-day, every step that I hear on the street,
 Seems to bring me a tiding of woe and despair;
Each ring at the door-bell my poor heart will beat,
 As if Jack, the dear boy, in his grave-clothes were there!
And I thought, when I saw you—I'm nervous and queer—
You had brought me some news it would kill me to hear.
Please don't be concerned, sir. I'm bound, that in spite
Of my foolish old fancies, the boy is all right.

"No, I don't think we'd sell. For it's this way, you see:
 Jack says that he never will care for the smile
Of a girl, till he knows she's in love, too, with me;
 And I tell him—ha! ha!—*that* will be a long while.
So we'll doubtless bide here a long time. And there's some
 Little chance of Jack's leaving the engine, ere long,
For a place in the shops, where they say he'll become
 A master mechanic—good sir, what is wrong?

"You are death-pale and trembling! Here! drink some more tea!
Say! why are you looking your pity at me?
What's that word in your face?—you've a message!—now find
Your tongue!—No?—I'll tear the truth out of your mind!
JACK'S HURT! Oh, how hard that you could not at first
 Let me know this black news! Say, where is he, and when
Can he come home with me? But my poor heart will burst,
 If you do not speak out! Speak, I pray you, again!
I can stand it; why, yonder 's his own cosey bed;
 I will get it all fixed;—oh, but I'm a good nurse!
His hospital's home! Here I'll pillow his head;
 I will bring him to life, be he better or worse!

"'YOU ARE DEATH-PALE AND TREMBLING!   HERE!   DRINK SOME MORE TEA!'"

Oh, I tell you, however disfigured he be,
What is left of the boy shall be saved, sir, for me!
Thank God for the chance, even!   Oh, won't I work
    For my poor wounded child!   And now let me be led
Where he is.   Do not fear!   I'll not falter or shrink!
    Turn your face to the light, sir.—O God!   JACK IS DEAD!"

THE FESTIVAL OF FAMILY REUNION.

The Festival of Family Reunion.

Jeanie.

How strange that we all should be here together!—
    So hard to expect, that bleak black day
    When your poor body was borne away,
  Through the dreary, though sunlit weather;
  Borne by bearers, slow but fleet,
  From the house of the tree-roofed street;
  Taken by men with solemn tread,
  And placed in the vault with the rest of the dead—
  That we would be ever again united,
  That your dark room would again be lighted!
  I heard the voice of the preacher, saying,
    "He is not dead! He has gone before!"
  I heard the hymns, the sobs, the praying,
    And tried to believe, and hope even more;
  But reason said, "Be strong and clever;
  March on and give him up forever!"
  His life has fallen into a sea
    Of other life ; a raindrop clung
    To a branch that over the ocean hung,
  And was a picture to you and me;
  You marked its delicate shape and glitter,
    And loved it well, and called it yours;
  But it fell in the great waves cold and bitter;
    So how can you say, "It still endures!"
  And Faith cowed down at command of reason,
  Hope crept away with a look of treason,
  And everything was bleak and cold
  As clouds when the winter day is old.

But then my tired-out heart said over
   Some words that once to it had been taught;
I found them within a Bible's cover,
   And comfort home to my heart they brought.
Yet still the living will wonder whether
They and the dead can meet together,
Still the others will wonder instead,
How the living can call them dead.
Now all of our band excepting one—
   And she most loving and most dear—
   Are met together, sojourning here;
But souls just with the earth-life done,
   Have told me Mother would soon be near.
She comes through the Gate of the Narrow Way;
   I will watch for her—I must not miss her—
I will be the first, this gala-day
   To cuddle her in my arms and kiss her!
Then I will lead her—Heaven's new star—
Where our brothers and sisters are;
Then I will make our father's eyes
Into a gleam of glad surprise!

Hugh.

But, sister, we know not just the hour
   When she will come; though faith be steady,
To say, it is not within our power,
   But Mother is here in Heaven already.
Even now, she may meet the others,
Talk with our father, sisters, brothers;
Now in the new-old home be waiting
Fondly our whereabouts debating,
As in the earthly times, when we,
Out for an afternoon of glee,
Came home late to the homestead nest.—
Of earth's angels brightest and best,
And most fitted for Heaven, she
Will feel more at home than we.
How do we know, but in this throng
We have passed her? Many and long

Gather the years since her embrace;
Maybe we would not know her face.

JEANIE (*reproachfully*).

Know her! Give me even so much
As her eye-gleam—her hand's sweet touch—
A tone of her voice—her step—nay, less!
Even the rustle of her dress—
And I would know her! But, 'tis late;
Hasten we on to the Narrow Gate!

SCENE II., *the same. Enter the spirit of an aged lady. She walks up and down as if looking for some one. The brother and sister pass on the opposite side of the street without seeing her.*

AGED LADY.

I am in Heaven!—in Love's metropolis,
Faith's resting-place, Hope's loftiest mountain-top;
Prayer's last request, Virtue's supreme reward;
The never-ceasing Harvest Home of Life!
Yet how its wonders daze and frighten me,
And put my earth-imaginings to shame!
'Tis what I thought, and yet not what I thought;
'Tis what I felt, and yet not what I felt;
'Tis what I knew, and yet not what I knew.
O Ruler of all realms, be good to me—
A plain old woman from that plain young world—
And if not pure enough to see thy face,
Or if too humble for thy voice and hand
(No wonder, coming from the least of stars),
Pray send me pilotage; for 'tis a state
Most strangely sad—this being lost in Heaven!

[JEANIE *and* HUGH *disappear in the distance without her seeing them. Enter a little girl, dressed in white.*

9

LITTLE GIRL (*clasping* AGED LADY's *hand*).

> Lady, as these domes you pass,
>> Just let loose from worldly being;
> Earth still, like a darkened glass,
>> For a moment dims your seeing.
> Soon Heaven's wonders you shall trace,
> Heart to heart, and face to face;
> Soon this City land explore,
>> Having learned, with sweet endeavor,
> How to learn and prosper more—
>> How to find new joys forever.
> Now, till from old fetters free,
> I your faithful guide will be.

AGED LADY

Thanks, modestly precocious maid of Heaven,
But I have many dear old friends in town—
Friends who have loved me—friends who would not wait
A moment if they knew I waited them.
Why! on the earth, for half a hundred years,
When I from distance-shadows reached home's light,
Friends met me with soft kisses and warm smiles;
And would they let this long, dark journey cease—
A journey they had taken, and so knew
What it would be—without even silent words
Of welcome—yes, a long and sweet embrace?
There's some mistake; they did not get the word!

LITTLE GIRL.

> God has undiscovered ways
>> Here within his narrow portals;
> Oh, they puzzle even the gaze
>> Of the wisest of immortals!
> Angels know not all His plan,
> Even on earth, with humble man;
> Much less, in this serial story,
> Of his god-bewildering glory!
> But, sweet lady, never fear;
>> No pure joy on earth is given,

"A GRAND OLD MANSION ON A CITY ROAD."

But, all glorified and clear,
  Can be reproduced in Heaven.

AGED LADY.

Oh, sweet-voiced girl, so wise beyond your years,
Are earthly houses e'er rebuilt in Heaven?

LITTLE GIRL.

There's no place where memory
  Goes for tidings good and pleasant,
None where love and purity
  Have been found, but here are present.
All best things on earth are mere
Shadow-copies cast from here;
All earth's good has, on this side,
It's original glorified.

AGED LADY.

Sweet girl, one time, that far-off earth contained
A grand old mansion on a city road,
Yet with its little field of lawn embraced—
A stately, prosperous pile, and still a home.
Vines nursed their pretty children of green leaves,
And buds, and flowers; and the well-guarded door
Reached out its brass hands for all those to shake
Who came with kind intent. No honest Want
E'er went away, except with grateful smile.
Sweet children raced and shouted through its halls,
And mimicked older life in sports and games;
Here hearts and hands clasped in true-thoughted love.
A thousand eves did hospitality
Light up those halls with kind and welcome guests,
'Mid floods of light and life and happiness.
But Time and greedy Commerce have pulled down
Our refuge, and have left of it no trace.
Great, huckstering shops are spread upon the lawn;
The world came past and swept our home away.
I have not even its picture for my eyes,
Though it has long been painted on my heart.

Think you that I might not see, just for once,
A picture of the dear old house in Heaven?

    LITTLE GIRL.

        Wishes are fulfilment here,
          When with God's desires agreeing;
        Turn and look; your home is near;
          Heaven in Heaven awaits your seeing.

        [*The* AGED LADY *turns and views the old house, evidently smiling recognition at her. She bursts into tears.*

    LITTLE GIRL.

        Joy should plume your heart with wings!
        Do you weep at pleasant things?

    AGED LADY.

Alas! on earth we do so learn to weep—
The habit even follows us through joy;
I thank you, angel girl—I thank Thee, God!
'Tis the old house once more—'tis Heaven in Heaven!

————

SCENE III., *A room in the new-found old mansion. The* AGED LADY *walking up and down, alone.*

    AGED LADY.

The same old home, in the Great Home restored!
Each loved hall's floor my practised feet have pressed;
All nooks and corners my glad hands have found;
My eyes have fed on each familiar scene.
All is the same! Restored—I must believe,
By well-taught angel hands—how faithfully!
And every room had tales to tell to me
Of loved old times; and every wall had tongues,
And talked a while about the dear dead days;
But ah, what empty rooms! Not one sweet face
Of all those loved ones! Oh, kind-hearted God,

Does loneliness pursue us even in Heaven?
Home ne'er was home when husband was not there!

*[A door opens and her husband enters. They rush
to each other's arms.*

HUSBAND.

You see, there were so many things
   That no one knew but we, dear—
So many sly heart-whisperings
   Had gone 'twixt you and me, dear!
So many thoughts, and all our own,
'Twas hardly Heaven to live alone,
Even with Heaven's glories round me strown!

You see, though friends all came this way,
   To grasp me by the hand, dear;
There was so much I wished to say,
   They could not understand, dear!
Though sympathy around me fell,
And my earth-woes were pitied well,
There was so much I could not tell!

Though friendship could not theirs excel
   In being kind and true, dear,
There was so much I could not tell
   To any one but you, dear!
It calls for Heaven's supremest art
To heal a warm and loving heart,
That from its half is crushed apart.

And so from Heaven I used to gaze
   Through fields of space afar, dear,
Upon the distant homesick rays
   Of one particular star, dear;
There ne'er was one of mortal birth
Looked more at stars of heavenly worth
Than I from Heaven gazed at earth.

There were so many things to see,
   Alone, I could not view, love!

Heaven's angels, they were good to me,
　But then, they were not you, love!
I wondered so that you could stay
So*many years from me away,
When my heart called you every day!

And one by one the children came:
　Each one had to bereave you;
And all were sad, though not with blame,
　So lonely they must leave you!
For while there is no sorrow here,
There may be yearnings, sweetly drear.
For cherished ones who come not near.

But now, once more, and face to face,
　In happiness we meet, wife;
And through your care and God's sweet grace
　Our family is complete, wife!
From valleys, mountains, snows, and sands,
From city streets and forest lands,
They come to clasp your yearning hands.

AGED LADY.

My children, children, children—are they here?

> [*A door opens, and five of her loved ones enter, con-
> ducted by the* LITTLE GIRL *guide, who then dis-
> appears.*

AGED LADY (*clasping them one after another*).

My loved, lost children! found, and found in Heaven!
Children and homestead both together found!
Now Heaven be praised, for Heaven is Heaven at last;
Now, once again, we learn that home is Heaven!

SCENE IV., *same.*

AGED LADY.

Come, let us camp around the family hearth,
And visit, as in those sun-gilded years,

When we were happiest; let once more our eyes
The watch-fires of old memories kindle bright;
Let's barter news for news, and thoughts for thoughts,
Play toss-ball with the old love-cushioned jokes,
And set the air to singing with our laughs.
And yet 'twould seem, oh, sweethearts of my prime,
As if, in these long, slow, oft-counted years,
You must have larger, stronger, older grown.
But here you meet me, young and blooming still,
Just as you seemed in our best, happiest days.
A miracle!

HUSBAND.
   All things are "miracles,"
Whether in earth or Heaven, till we have found
Their law and reason. Early here we learn
That wishes oft are their accomplishment.

AGED LADY.
And yet I grieve that you, being all so young,
Must meet the mother, crookèd, bent, and worn,
And not so comely as she was of old;
For, trust me, I was not so hideous then,
And had, I fear, some sinful worldly pride.
      [*All the others laugh merrily.*
HUSBAND.
There was a picture in our dear old house,
That I sometimes have seen you glance upon;
View it once more for me, and tell me true
If 'tis as then. Look in yon gilded frame.

   [AGED LADY *turns, and gazes, where he points, into*
   a mirror. She sees herself reflected as a beauti-
   ful middle-aged woman. All laugh, pettingly, at
   her surprise.
HUSBAND.
The earthly count of years counts not in Heaven;
All are as one in everlasting prime,
Free from youth's follies and the bars of age;
Though each may change appearance as he likes,

And as shall suit his Heaven-born purposes—
From old to young, or young to old. The soul
Can often change the body's looks on earth;
A million times as much the spirit-form!

———

SCENE V., *library of the mansion.   Parents and children assemble for
    prayers.*

MOTHER.

It seems so strange to pray, now we are given
So much we toiled and prayed for! Still, true prayers
Are partly thanks; and though each separate one
Reached through eternity—and it were then
By millions and by millions multiplied—
'Twere not enough to give our God for Heaven;
And 'tis our duty, from this vantage-ground,
To plead for those who suffer still on earth.

HUSBAND.

You know it was a favorite plan of ours,
In each day's first-formed prayer, to counsel well
What I should ask for; oft thus giving aim
To the petition; let us counsel now.

WIFE.

Good customs wear but brighter with the years.
How sweet that good devices ne'er grow old!
Yes, I have prayers—thousands of silent prayers—
That I would love to have you lend a voice,
And proffer for me, even here in Heaven:
For misled mortals, who on earth still creep
Through thorns of others' wretchedness and vice:
For mothers, in eternities of pangs;
For fathers, in proud, sad solicitude;
For youths and maidens, when temptation smiles;
For those who struggle in disease's clutch;
For those who strangle in the sloughs of crime;
For ships that fight through battles of the storms,
And mortals clinging to their dripping sides:

For wrecked ones, hanging to the ocean's top;
For toilers, stifling in blockaded mines;
For wayward feet that led hearts into fire;
For mangled forms beneath unflinching wheels;
For those who starve, with treasures round them stored;
For those whose blood has rusted murderers' knives—
Much more for murderers with crime-rusted souls;
For those who breathe the fogs of pestilence;
For prisoners in unjustly-welded chains—
Still more for those whose punishment is just;
For sick ones—hating life and dreading death;
For mourners with their wounded hearts entombed;
For suffering every way and everywhere;
Nay, if it be not wrong—for spirits lost!

HUSBAND.

The same sweet soul, with pity in each throb!
And for yourself, can you no favor ask,
Or (as pure wish in Heaven for one's self
Is the accomplishment) can you not tell
Of some dear want, which, if it has been met,
You know not of the granting?

WIFE.   Husband mine,
You know the babe that lived but one short hour;
She was our last bud from the vines of Heaven.
And I, 'mid throes of pain, was comforted,
Because, I mused, her sweet and winsome heart
Would cherish me when our dear older ones
Had grown away from us. But one short hour—
One hope-strewn, fear-strewn, pain-strewn hour—she lived.
How much I have been thinking of her, dear—
Have longed for her! Say, have you ever seen
This sweet-breathed baby of our later love?
I yearn so sadly for her!

[*Enter the* LITTLE GIRL *guide, and rushes into the
mother's arms.*

LITTLE GIRL.
                I am she.

Notes.

1 "Early in the following March (1677), the Quaker proprietors completed and published a body of laws under the singular title of Concessions. But the name was significant, for everything was accorded to the people. The first simple code enacted by the Friends in America rivalled the charter of Connecticut in the liberality and purity of its principles. . . . The doctrines of the Concessions were reaffirmed. Men of all races and of all religions were declared to be equal before the law. No superiority was conceded to rank or title, to wealth or royal birth."—Ridpath's *History of the United States.*

2 This poem was first read by the author at a reunion of the Army of the Potomac, in Orange, New Jersey, and the line

"Traced over these hills its eager track,"

alludes to General McClellan's love of New Jersey, his last earthly home.

3 Whoever has viewed the features of Stonewall Jackson in life, in marble, or even the most ordinary portrait, must have been struck by the kindness and sweetness of their expression.

4 It has been reserved for a miniature South American republic, whose interests should be the same as ours, to excite the hostility and war spirit which resulted in some improvement to our navy.

5 The Council at Salamanca, in 1486, to decide whether it was best to furnish Columbus with a few ships and men for the possible discovery of land in the Far West, was, all things considered, one of the most interesting to be found in history. The idea of this obscure and poverty-stricken mariner seems to have struck most of these wise men of Spain about as favorably as would a proposed colonization of the moon. Nearly all of them were at first piously but bitterly against him. Fernando de Talavera, who presided, was prior of the monastery of Prado, Confessor to Queen Isabella, and considered one of the best educated men of the time. He was prejudiced against the new enterprise. Diego de Deza, who appears in the Council as Columbus' friend, was at that time a professor of theology in the Convent of St. Stephen, and afterwards Archbishop of Seville. He was also a man of liberal education for those days, but had not permitted his common-sense and liberality of mind to become impaired in the process. As Irving says, with his combination of truth and elegance, he "was a man whose mind was above the narrow bigotry of bookish lore: one who could appreciate the value of wisdom, even when uttered by unlearned lips." He assisted Columbus with his purse during days of poverty, and contributed toward the enterprise the jewels of his mind as lavishly as Isabella did those of her caskets. Had it not been for his help it is very doubtful whether the schemes of Columbus could have been pushed forward to success. The remainder of this Council, "professors of astronomy, geography, mathematics, and other branches of science, together with various dignitaries of the church and learned friars," were most of them deeply prejudiced against the needy Italian adventurer.

6 Alluding to the wife of the discoverer, whom, his enemies declare, he deserted and neglected during his prosperity.

7 It was one of Columbus' most cherished projects to use a part of the riches acquired by the contemplated discoveries toward raising armies for the recovery of the holy sepulchre in Palestine.

[*] Columbus offered to whomever of his crew might first discover land a doublet of velvet. There had also been offered a pension by Ferdinand and Isabella. About ten o'clock one evening Columbus thought he saw a light in the distance which might proceed from some torch or lantern upon the land. He called a witness to view it with him, but they saw only occasional flashes of it afterwards. They were not considered at the time as indicating land by any one except Columbus, who evidently exhibited, at this time as at others, the superiority of his judgement over those who associated with him. At two the next morning land was discovered by Roger de Triana, a common sailor, who claimed the doublet and the pension; but the rewards were given to Columbus, on account of his having perceived the lights. The historical enemies of Columbus, of whom there are many, have loudly denounced the action of Columbus in thus taking away the pension from a poor sailor, some of them asserting that he did it "to increase his revenue;" but it is likely that he cared more for the honor of the achievement than for any financial benefit to be derived from it. The poor mariner Triana is said to have been so disgusted at the decision against him that he renounced his country and his religious faith, went to Africa, and became a Mohammedan.

[*] All of which (supposititious) curses were literally fulfilled.

[10] The term "Scientist" is employed in this poem as with no idea of reproach toward the scientists of the present day, who, it is needless to say, are of an entirely different class from those of the time of Columbus, and generally at the lead of all discovery and progress.

[11] Alluding to the story that Columbus received his first ideas of land to westward from an old pilot who, in 1484, eight years previous to the voyage from Palos, had died in his house at Terceras, had left him all his charts and log-books, containing an account of his having been driven westward upon a recent voyage until he found an island (claimed to have been the present San Domingo). This story has been exploded again and again, but is still brought up to the discredit of Columbus, and will probably always be, according to the (fictitious) hag's prophecy.

[12] The Spirit of Progress had evidently here a prophetic vision of the Columbian Exposition, to take place at Chicago, four hundred years later.

[13] It has been said that everybody is, to some extent, a freak of nature, and there is certainly much gold of truth in this nugget of a remark. We are all peculiar, not to say queer, in some way, and the only advantage, perhaps, that we have over the regularly recognized freaks, is, that we can conceal the peculiarities of mind which they have to display in the body. There are, as we know, many *mental* living skeletons, bearded ladies, dwarfs, armless men, "what-is-its," etc., etc., and it is interesting and rather mournful to contemplate that in the course of generations these intellectual peculiarities may, perhaps, develop into regular physical freaks. So we must not consider these queer people whom we see at the museums as a separate race. They are for the most part intensely human, and appreciate good and kindly treatment from their curiosity-seeking brothers and sisters. Many of them toil at the wearying, laborious, and oftimes humiliating profession of exhibiting themselves, because it is the only means they possess of earning a living. Most of them support families and friends, who, by being, unfortunately, in possession of all their limbs, in good and proper shape, are unable to earn a subsistence for themselves. No wonder that the "freaks" wish to have a little festival of their own once in a while—to mingle in a social gathering in which no one of them is conspicuous, and all are comrades, in full and equal standing.

[14] "Hey Reub!" is the show-man's war-cry; and he is bound in honor to rush to the support of any of his comrades who by this means indicates that he is engaged in pugilistic conflict with some member of the general public.

[15] The first rails used in this country for the running of railroad cars were not steel, as at present, nor even iron, but of the tougher species of wood.

[16] The number of railroad accidents in which employés are maimed and killed is appalling. It has been estimated that the casualties thus resulting on the different railroads of the United States each year equal in number those of the Battle of Waterloo or of Gettysburg.